Extra Volume

Falling

An imprint of Via Lactea Ltd.

Author: Yu Cheng
Translators: Arien; Yun; Hobbitsflower
Editor: Moca
Proofreader: OWL
Layout Designer: Ayan

CONTACT:
Customer Support: info@vialactea.ca
Wholesale & Distribution: market@vialactea.ca
Other Cooperation: https://vialactea.ca/pages/cooperation
Discord Channel: https://discord.gg/vialactea

Follow us on X/Instagram/Facebook: @ViaLactea_Ltd
Official Website: www.vialactea.ca

ISBN 978-1-77408-523-3 (pbk)
Printed in Canada

LOCATION:
Shops At Waterloo Town Square
#27, 75 King Street South, Waterloo, ON
Canada
N2J 1P2

A teacher for a day,
a husband for life.

CONTENT

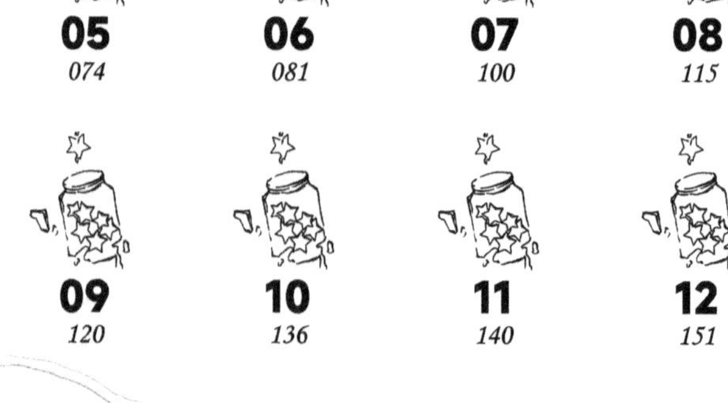

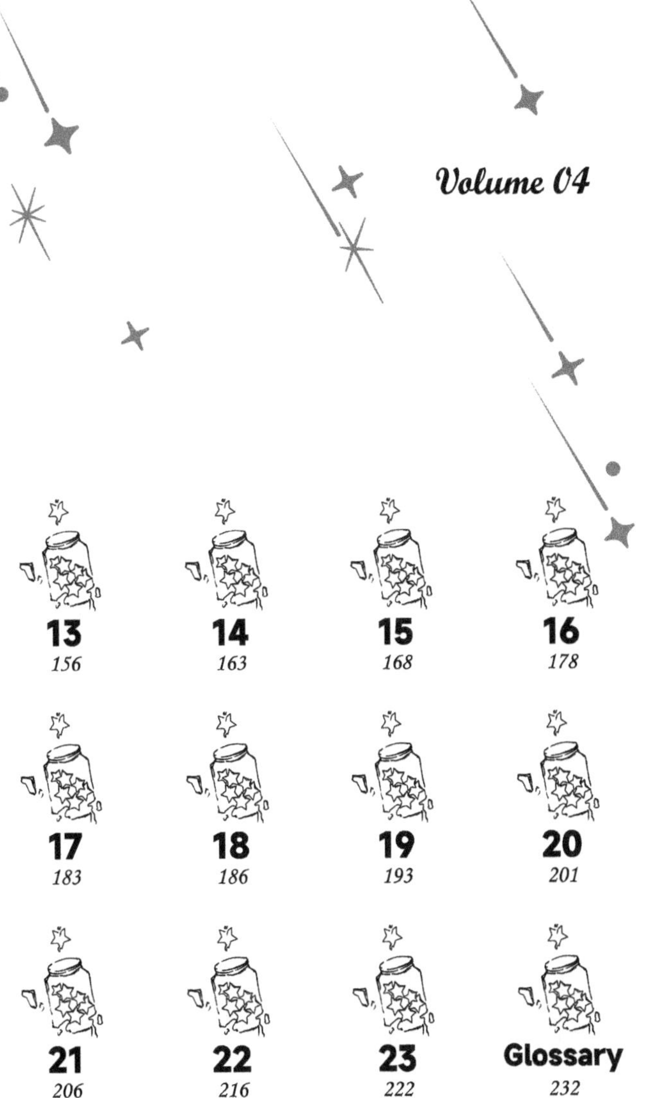

Falling

Extra Volume

EXTRA 01

The Sixth Year

THAT day, Cheng Feichi went back to the capital from S-City under the excuse of collecting stuff. He stayed by himself in the already emptied apartment for half an hour.

As he rushed to the airport, he answered Yi Zheng's call. He began with some questions out of fatherly concern, and followed with, "If your dad didn't donate to ensure your success, you wouldn't have been able to get into that school. When you get there, get rid of any distractions and study properly. Aim to graduate and come back as soon as possible. Don't make your mother worry."

These few simple sentences were rich with implicit meaning: *Everything you've achieved was because of my support. Don't forget what you promised me. From today on, do what you should do and let go of any concerns you shouldn't have.*

As he hung up, the car was passing through High School No. 6. Today was the first day of school. Through the wide iron gates, there was an orderly array of students on the schoolyard, presumably holding the opening assembly.

Cheng Feichi simply swept them an indifferent glance before looking away.

Though Yi Zheng's worry wasn't unjustified, it was still somewhat unnecessary.

He was never someone who would dwell on the past. The world was constantly changing, and so was one's life. He never regretted what he did, and more than that, he could never go back.

In the first year, Cheng Feichi took half a year of language courses.

As he had gone abroad in a hurry, he didn't have IELT scores. Thankfully, he had a pretty good foundation of English and graduated from his language courses just in time for the fall term. Yi Zheng provided him an ample amount for living expenses, but he was used to being frugal. Rather than getting a studio, he shared an ensuite apartment with several students.

All of the local students liked to socialize, and the noisy hubbub inside their rooms could often be heard just by standing outside the door. This was especially so on the weekends, where the dorm parties lasted through the night. Thus, Cheng Feichi spent most of his time in school. He carried his notebooks in his backpack and went to the library to continue studying right after class, only returning at night to sleep.

He kept to himself. He was usually never seen in the dorm and didn't participate in any of the various parties. As time went by, he became transparent in his classmates' eyes.

Towards this, he had no opinions. Changing one's country was no more than changing a common language. To him, life was no different than before. He had never been scared of loneliness.

On the contrary, getting Yi Hui's calls once in a while made him feel suddenly pulled back to reality.

For instance, on the day before Christmas Eve of this year, the school and dorms were adorned with colorful lights and Christmas trees everywhere, yet Yi Hui said over the phone,

"Today's the Winter Solstice. Did you eat glutinous rice balls?"

It was already night on Cheng Feichi's end. He was taken aback and his hand froze in the middle of turning a page. After letting this set in for a bit, he said, "No, there are no glutinous rice balls here."

"Then what about dumplings? Mom said dumplings are good too."

"No dumplings either."

"Ah...how sad," Yi Hui sighed. "When you come back, I'll treat you to glutinous rice balls and dumplings!"

On the way back from the classroom, snow suddenly fell from the dark skies. Several Chinese students making the journey stopped excitedly to take pictures. To most people, nothing was a more fitting match than snow and Christmas.

Perhaps because he was affected by them, Cheng Feichi halted his steps and looked at the snowflakes fluttering down to the ground. Suddenly, there was a voice in his ears asking him if he knew what day today was.

The crisp, clear voice, like an echo from the depths of a cliff, should have been as light and soft as the snow, yet it stabbed a sharp pain into Cheng Feichi's heart. He lifted his steps and walked against the gradually heavier snow, not pausing for a moment.

In the second year, because Yan Hong showed up, Cheng Feichi's social life had a slight change.

At first, he didn't know why this girl bothered him all the time. He saw her everywhere: in the classroom, the library, the dormitory. It wasn't until he got a phone call from his mother, Cheng Xin, and then received a similar call from Yi Zheng—telling him to look after Yan Hong, and to visit and get close to her—that he realized the stakes involved.

Even if she was put in a school with groups of people of every

color, Yan Hong was still an eye-catching presence. Her good family background and a cheerful personality ensured she had no lack of suitors.

Because her suitors were persistent, Cheng Feichi, who had originally been taciturn, also received attention. Rumors spread one after another. The gossip of him being an illegitimate son also began to spread far and wide amongst the local Chinese exchange students.

At first, they only dared to make insinuations behind his back. After Yi Zheng's original wife came to "visit" the school in broad daylight for the second time, everyone knew Cheng Feichi's identity. As a result, no one held back anymore. Cheng Feichi received ridicule and rejection directly to his face four or five times.

Cheng Xin often called to ask about his studies and life. There were so many opportunities, but Cheng Feichi never told her about these issues. At first, he thought there was no need. He had experienced this kind of thing many times from a young age. He'd long been able to expressionlessly let things go in one ear and out the other.

Besides, what they were saying was true. He had no grounds for denial.

Cheng Feichi once used this as an excuse to reject Yan Hong and have her choose one of the truly rich and powerful heirs. Yan Hong didn't agree and sought him out time after time, telling him that she didn't like anyone else, only him.

Her relentless pursuit almost made Cheng Feichi think of another person.

But this idea hadn't fully formed in his head before he consciously changed his focus, preventing himself from having that thought.

In the end, he rejected Yan Hong.

His heart was too small. It couldn't even seal off the memories, let alone hold anyone else.

In the third year, Cheng Feichi crammed courses in order to fast-track to graduate school and was so busy that he only got four to five hours of sleep every day.

Cheng Xin's health steadily deteriorated, particularly in the winter. From over the phone, he could tell that her voice was weak and that she was listless.

In this year, the only recreational activity that Cheng Feichi participated in was the Great Lego Contest in that state.

The dormmate next door came from S-City and had traveled back to China for Christmas, bringing back half a suitcase of chili peppers. He forcefully gave him a bundle, telling him they were called "Er Jing Tiao" and paired well with BBQ chicken, duck, or rabbit.

He used them to make a fish dish. The fragrance beckoned the majority of students in the dormitory. Everyone sat around a table, taking a bite here and a spoonful there, chit-chatting until the topic fell on next month's Great Lego Contest. Surrounded by a crowd that ganged up on him from left and right, Cheng Feichi, who barely ever participated in group activities, finally agreed to join to save face.

At the contest site, he ran into an old acquaintance. When Zhao Yue saw him, he even came over and said hello. Seeing his cold reaction and refusal to chat, Zhao Yue lost interest and left moodily.

After they started stacking the pieces, Cheng Feichi found out that they wanted to use the machinery blueprint that he had once drawn up. He immediately refused.

"Even if you gave it away, you still made it. You're the owner of this blueprint," one of the students urged. "We're just using it

to participate in the contest. No one will know."

Cheng Feichi still refused.

"Since I already gave it to him, that blueprint belongs to him alone." Cheng Feichi's eyes stayed on the blueprint from start to finish. "I don't have the right to take back his things without his approval."

In the fourth year, Cheng Feichi started his master's degree.

One night, he got a phone call from the caretaker who was looking after Cheng Xin. "Can you come back to see her? The madam is very sick. She was calling your name in her dreams."

As soon as Cheng Feichi hung up, he opened his computer to book a flight ticket. His card got stuck on check-out each time, with the monitor repeatedly displaying an insufficient balance. He took his card to swipe at the self-serve ATM, and likewise, couldn't take out money. It had all been frozen, including the money that he had saved up from working several concurrent jobs.

He called Yi Zheng and left messages, but didn't get a response for the entire night. Cheng Feichi had a hunch that this was some scheme worked up by *that* woman, but he couldn't wait, afraid that Cheng Xin really would pass away suddenly. Helpless, he could only borrow money from his classmates.

The timing was bad. The few classmates he was familiar with had gone on vacation together to a bordering country, and couldn't be reached in a short period of time. Cheng Feichi turned around and went to borrow from the Chinese students in the next dorm, promising to return the money as soon as he came back to the country.

His fellow student didn't decline the request. With a draped-on smile, he had Cheng Feichi wait a while at the door. Not long after, laughter echoed from the dorm. Cheng Feichi caught a few phrases, pretty much all ridicule—suggesting that

the reason he was in such a hurry to go back was to for the real young master of the Yi family to ride him like a horse.

Neither getting angry nor contradicting them, he waited until they finished mocking him and sloppily tossed him some money. Under the eyes of an entire house of jeering people, he told them politely, "Thank you."

He rushed back to China, and Cheng Xin, lying on the hospital bed, was both surprised and panicked as she saw him. She demanded why he came back and wanted him to go back to study at once, and to not let Yi Zheng hear about this by any means.

Seeing that his mother was fine, Cheng Feichi gave a breath of relief. He had just gotten off a sixteen-hour long-distance flight when he was urged back to the airport by Cheng Xin. He also lacked strength to pursue the deceitful affair and the frozen debit card.

On the way, he peered out the window at the motherland that he'd been estranged from for three years. It was a pity that many buildings on S-City's streets were different from the capital's; he felt no attachment to them. He gave a few casual glances and looked away.

He never imagined that he would see *him* on the bus's TV screen.

His appearance was always so unforeseen that Cheng Feichi couldn't even evade it in time, despite wanting to.

That radiant smiling face appeared in an ad, in a contorted pose, speaking awkward scripted lines. Cheng Feichi subconsciously looked away, but for some unknown reason, he forced himself to stare straight at the screen, as if using this to prove that he didn't care.

When the ad finished, he turned his head and looked out the window.

This time he gazed steadily, focusing, as if wanting to etch the

roadside scenery into his brain and thus shut out everything else.

The fifth year was the busiest.

There were infinite theses, reports, and seminars. Cheng Feichi wanted to pass his defense, graduate, and go back to China. Four years ago, when he first stepped foot on this land, he allowed himself five years, no more and no less.

Yan Hong made a fuss about going back to China with him, even abandoning the opportunity to go to graduate school for this. Cheng Feichi didn't approve, but she said, unperturbed, "There's no use if I study so much. I won't inherit the family business. Just let me slack off."

This move made people around them further confirm that the two of them were a couple. Unable to explain, Cheng Feichi simply responded with silence. When they chewed their tongues off, unable to dig up any information, they would naturally lose interest and let it go.

As soon as a person became busy, they wouldn't have time to mind other stuff around them. Cheng Feichi preferred this kind of state that allowed him to wholeheartedly immerse himself into his studies.

Elite families cared most about blood relations and degrees of kinship. How could they let their own bloodline carry someone else's last name? Cheng Feichi was obviously an outsider.

There weren't a lot of people close to him in the first place. Even if he had never personally announced his identity in public, this kind of thing passed through the grapevine exponentially quickly nowadays and was taken as the truth even when that might not necessarily be the case. In a flash, the rumor that "Cheng Feichi is pretending to be the Yi family's young master" was everywhere. Half the people pitied him, and the other half mocked his vanity, rubbing salt into the wound.

If it were just a couple of people who hated him, he wouldn't have paid them any mind, but this affair even reached his advisor's ears. His advisor, who was dedicated wholeheartedly to academia, hated it most when students lied about their backgrounds and sent back his thesis at once. Putting on a stern face, he told Cheng Feichi to correct his character before thinking of graduating.

During these years, Cheng Feichi was occupied with school-work, becoming more and more silent. Apart from obligated interactions during classes, he could even go a whole day without saying anything.

But on that day, for the first time, he said a lot. He didn't say one word about his family affairs, but rather argued his thesis from beginning to end to his advisor. At first, his advisor wanted to cut him off; unable to manage that, he could only listen to him finish.

Cheng Feichi had a very upright approach to his studies, never trying to introduce fluff to his thesis just to be done with it. His advisor gradually began to listen. After he finished, he muttered under his breath for a moment, then took the initiative to apologize for his biased attitude and flawed understanding of the facts.

In the end, to lighten the mood, his advisor asked him jokingly why he was in such a hurry to go back to China. It couldn't be that he had a young and beautiful wife waiting for him at home, right?

Cheng Feichi blanked out for a moment. A face he hadn't recalled for a long time flashed before his eyes.

But it was just a quick flash, so quick that the image hadn't had time to reach his central nervous system before it scattered.

Cheng Feichi looked down, summoning an excuse that he had used many times. "I have a sick mother at home."

After many ups and downs, he finally graduated smoothly in the summer of the sixth year.

Cheng Feichi didn't return to the capital. He went straight to S-City to take on the job that Yi Zheng gave him.

This was the agreement they had reached five years ago: Yi Zheng would allow him to study abroad, whereas he would help manage the family business.

The media in China had keen noses. Shortly after Cheng Feichi returned, he was secretly followed and photographed, and those were then spread online. When the masses had nothing to do, they loved to see strange news in the entertainment circle or snoop into stories of the rich and famous. The conglomerate's public relations team had a hard job, as they were tasked with investigating and managing suspected rumors.

One time, because they couldn't reach a decision, the public relations team reported a piece of content up the hierarchy. Cheng Feichi had a look at it, and this time, the site where the rumors had originated was actually the forum of Beijing's High School No. 6.

When he studied at High School No. 6, he had never gone on this forum, and the only recognition he had towards it came from Ye Qin.

Cheng Feichi was astonished that he could so calmly recall that name. He thought that he had hidden it very deeply, so that even if it was suddenly mentioned someday, his heart would no longer stir up any waves.

He offhandedly flipped through the post containing pictures of him searching through the hotel on it. Among them, there were two where Yan Hong was accidentally captured. Even without looking, he knew what the comments were debating. Cheng Feichi closed the page and said to the PA, "It's just a school forum with very few visitors, no need to worry about it."

He also dealt with a few messages being spread on Weibo and set the boundaries on how public relations would deal with similar problems henceforth. The personal assistant picked up files, about to leave, when Cheng Feichi called out to her.

"After someone becomes a celebrity...I'm talking about actors or singers; can you see them on Weibo?"

The personal assistant had only worked with this new boss who had come back from overseas for half a month. Not very familiar with his tendencies and working style, she pondered a moment and then gave a guarded answer. "Yes. Usually, artists open up their own Weibo accounts. You just have to search that artist's name on Weibo and you can follow their daily activity."

After the personal assistant left, Cheng Feichi picked up his phone and opened the Weibo app that he had just closed not long ago. His thumb hovered on the screen for a good while. In the end, he didn't type anything in the search bar.

After that, for a period of time that was neither long nor short, Cheng Feichi remained in this confounding situation.

Reuniting with Ye Qin was both outside of his expectations, yet also somehow made him feel that it was all a matter of course.

He froze everything around him into ice and stayed on a remote, uninhabited island for a full five years. He thought he would always remain like this, but from the first time that he saw Ye Qin, all the problems and conflicts that should have never arisen for him smashed out like a tide. In an instant, it drowned the island all at once, as if wanting to make up for what had been missing for five years.

On that day, the elevator trapped them in a tiny, cramped space. Ye Qin forced back his tears, explaining to him how he'd accidentally stumbled into him after their reunion again and again.

In that cold, dark corner, Cheng Feichi was likewise review-

ing the course of events that had caused a steadily traveling train to once again go off the rails.

The first time, he had only just entered the room when he saw Ye Qin.

After the song began, even if he didn't look, he could still tell Ye Qin's voice apart from the other two singers.

Later on, a person left halfway and Ye Qin sat beside him. He saw several times that the hand Ye Qin used to drink water was shaking, particularly when someone sitting at the table asked about his left-handedness. Ye Qin's fingertips, pressing on the cup, turned white from force. And then he almost choked on a gulp of water, covered his mouth, turned away and coughed heavily.

Cheng Feichi thought that he didn't care. At the end of the event, his steps when leaving were as firm as ever, yet just before getting in the car, he found that his phone was not on him.

The second time, Cheng Xin was careless when getting up from her wheelchair and fell. The new caretaker who had just started not long ago called him. He set aside his work and rushed over—recently, they had chosen a public hospital less than two kilometers from her residence.

When he ran into Ye Qin, he was lining up to get pictures from the X-ray machine. The ambulance had stopped at the entrance and doctors and nurses rushed like mad to push the critical patient inside. Ye Qin stood in place and looked on stupidly for a while before stepping back, tripping on the shoe-laces that he hadn't tied properly.

It was completely on instinct that Cheng Feichi helped steady him. The small talk he had with Ye Qin afterwards was also out of politeness. He heard that Ye Qin had hurt his tailbone from skating. Cheng Feichi originally wanted to ask him why

he came to the hospital by himself, but as he was on the verge of speaking, he felt that it wasn't suitable and, in the end, replaced it with a hum.

The third time was right when Cheng Feichi brought his mother back to the capital to visit his grandmother and grandfather. Just as he installed his old SIM card, the phone suddenly rang.

Even if there wasn't that saved number, he could tell who this number belonged to in under a second. He had once ignored this number. Later, it was at Ye Qin's repeated insistence that he fixed his "bad habit" of not picking up the phone and not texting back in a timely fashion. Picking up this call was entirely a subconscious action.

Only, he never thought that he would hear the sound of crying.

He could be sure that Ye Qin was crying. Ye Qin loved his reputation, and never cried aloud. He could only guess from the rate of his breaths and the sound of his voice.

If the rapid breathing alone wasn't enough proof, that choked, "I miss you so much, gege," not only proved that he was crying but further became a hand that gripped his heart, making Cheng Feichi's heart shake, and making him blank out for a long time.

Who knew that Ye Qin came like a tumultuous storm, but left without a sound. He only left a disjointed, courteous note, tucked beneath a bottle of cologne to stop it from being blown away.

From then on, for Cheng Feichi, every meeting became a play full of twists and turns.

The fourth time, he became angry for reasons that he himself couldn't figure out.

Perhaps it was seeing Ye Qin leave the room Tang Chong booked, perhaps it was because Ye Qin diverted his eyes when he

saw him, or perhaps it was his overtly careful bearing sitting in the car, even taking out makeup from his pocket.

Cheng Feichi discovered that he also threw inexplicable fits at times. He felt helpless in this knowledge. He didn't want to be controlled or swayed, and merely pressed his lips together in silence, suppressing this bout of unease that had no cause and nowhere to dispel.

When a person has lived alone for a long time, it is difficult to avoid becoming stuck in their ways, or even becoming headstrong and stubborn.

Cheng Feichi originally thought that strange irritation would dispel with the passing of time. Who would have thought that it not only didn't, but also became more and more concentrated in places that he couldn't see. Finally, when Ye Qin spoke of "the fifth time," it was punctured by a sharp needle in an earth-shaking explosion.

He lost control. He couldn't see his own expression, but he must have looked violent and hateful. Otherwise, he wouldn't have scared Ye Qin to until his eyes turned red.

All his calmness and composure was torn into pieces at that moment. Drunkenness couldn't even be used as an excuse to hide behind.

For a few seconds, he even blamed his loss of control on Ye Qin.

Afterwards, he finally realized that he was never as magnanimous and tolerant as he believed. The deeper his love, the more resentful he became, and this hatred was a disfiguring drug.

In the game of love, he longed for the affection that he gave to be returned, longed for the sun to shine on his dark, damp shell.

His efforts were never selfless. He never wanted to become an individualist in others' eyes, just like he disliked the labels of "illegitimate child," "straight-A student," and the like.

Just like how he desperately tried to draw sunlight from Ye Qin, in order to become someone with warmth and a heartbeat.

Towards the end of the sixth year, because a certain someone often forgot his keys and had to squat outside and freeze, Cheng Feichi took the initiative, switching the normal lock in his home to a fingerprint lock.

Ye Qin's skill at hands-on work was simply okay. Folding 520 stars was already his limit. From start to finish, he practically offered no help, simply carrying the toolbox and standing to the side, waiting for orders.

The new keyhole was in a different position than the old one, so the installation took more effort. To save time, as soon as the door was set in place, Ye Qin went ahead to set the password. He stood outside, pressing "*beep, beep, beep*" and sticking his head in from time to time to see how far Cheng Feichi was with the installation.

After following the instruction manual until he could no longer, Ye Qin clutched the door with both hands and peeped out two round eyes. "The password... What should I set as the password?"

Tightening a screw, Cheng Feichi didn't raise his head. "Whatever you want."

Ye Qin shrank his head back. After a while, he mumbled across the door, "Then...is 0215 okay?"

Cheng Feichi raised his eyelids and replied, "Good."

When the lock was installed, Ye Qin volunteered to be the first to try. He had Cheng Feichi lock the door from inside the house to see if he could get in without a hitch.

As the door was about to close, Ye Qin, standing outside, suddenly lifted a hand and blocked it. "Wait."

Cheng Feichi looked at him through the crack in the door.

"What is it?"

Ye Qin struggled for a while and decided that he had to say it. He raised his head and looked at him bashfully, eyes seeming to shine with wetness. "If...if it doesn't open, you have to open the door for me... Don't shut me out."

Cheng Feichi was taken aback at first, but then smiled and nodded. "Okay, I'll open up for you."

Apart from what took place in the five years they were separated, there were a lot of things that Ye Qin didn't know.

For instance, the meaning of 0215. He stupidly gave this date another meaning, and even went ahead to use this sequence of numbers to warn himself.

For instance, he didn't know that on the day he cried extremely unattractively, Cheng Feichi actually opened the door and stood in the place he'd squatted from night the way into the morning.

For instance, he thought that when Cheng Feichi had left, he had thoroughly abandoned him and expelled him from his heart. Only until recently did that tightly shut door open a tiny sliver under his persistent pestering.

Little did he imagine that there was no need for anyone to open the door. Six years ago, he'd already taken root in Cheng Feichi's heart. Those roots grew downward, digging themselves deeper year after year.

He was like an unremovable sprout, and a sun that couldn't be hidden away by dark clouds. In every form, he stayed behind in this small world that belonged to him alone, one that he had never left.

EXTRA 02

I'm Willing

IN the autumn of that year, Ye Qin underwent a minor surgery to take out the steel plate stabilizing his left leg.

Without saying a word, Cheng Feichi arranged a private hospital room for him for half a month, making up for all the time that he didn't stay in the hospital when he had first broken it. After coming out from the surgical room, Ye Qin lived in a cycle of eating and sleeping, sleeping and eating. In less than a week, he already felt that he had put on weight.

Since his leg was injured, he couldn't move it substantially. Ye Qin made use of every moment of his limited ability to get up from the bed and walk around.

One time, he was splayed in front of the window, bathing in the wind and sun, when he heard the sound of footsteps and immediately scrambled back on the hospital bed like a monkey. When Cheng Feichi pushed open the door, he was still crawling on. Chen Feichi asked him what he was doing, and he pulled out a script from underneath the covers.

"Memorizing lines for an argument. It's a very heated one."

Cheng Feichi put down his things and reached out to take it. "Let me see how heated."

Ye Qin reluctantly handed him the script. Cheng Feichi gave it a cursory flip-through. Seeing something, the corner of his lips hooked up in a cryptic smile. "Yes, this is pretty heated."

Ye Qin took it back and took a look. The script was open to the pages where the second male lead passionately tried to pursue the female lead, sending her both flowers and breakfast. This made him unable to help recalling some past events, which were so embarrassing that his face heated up. He said bashfully, "This is just acting. I'm not really trying to pursue her."

Cheng Feichi lifted his eyebrows. "You really want to pursue her?"

"No!" In his passion, Ye Qin pulled down the script blocking his face. Then, he didn't know where to look, eyes flitting everywhere. His voice went weak. "I've only ever tried to pursue...super, super, super heatedly."

Cheng Feichi smiled deeper. He turned and came back, petting Ye Qin's hair that had been blown into disarray by the wind. "I know. Rest well. Don't wander around."

Ye Qin felt like he was probably a monkey in Cheng Feichi's eyes, there just to make him smile. It had been like that before, and it was still like that now.

Especially when he thought back to their first date. Such a funny movie couldn't make him smile, wasn't even as good as a passing comment from Ye Qin. When Ye Qin thought of this, he felt both happy and complicated; happy that he was uniquely special, and complicated that the meaning behind his words and actions were seen through so clearly by Cheng Feichi.

Although there wasn't anything bad about that, he had too much free time lately and kept on pondering it, thinking that he suffered a bit of a loss.

Because he could never tell what Cheng Feichi was thinking

unless Cheng Feichi was willing to put it out in the open.

For example, last week Cheng Feichi was clearly busier than before, only staying for a short period of time in the hospital room before leaving. He didn't stay overnight either, and when Ye Qin asked him what he was doing, he just said it was work.

Ye Qin wasn't stupid. Work? Where, in the middle of the night?

Yesterday, he didn't come at all, instead instructing his personal assistant to deliver pork bone soup. Ye Qin vaguely asked after him, but the personal assistant remained tight-lipped. "Knowing President Cheng's activities outside of work isn't within in my scope of duties."

Ye Qin wore a cheery expression, but he later narrowed his eyes and thought, *I knew it! You're not really at work! You're hiding something from me!*

The next day, Cheng Feichi came, but as usual, only sat for a while before leaving. Ye Qin sat on the bed, sending him off with his eyes. He counted to ten silently and then leapt out of the bed in a rustle, edging out of the room. He tiptoed after Cheng Feichi down the stairs, around one corner and another, and then...saw him go into the opposite hospital building.

After waiting until he was sure that Cheng Feichi had left the hospital, Ye Qin returned to the hospital room that he had just left. Two nurses were pushing a small cart packed with medication.

He stood at the doorway and peered at the scene inside. It was a similar one-person hospital room. A ventilator and heart monitor displaying the patient's poor health were displayed bedside. Even overlaid with a blanket, he could see that the patient had suffered from their illness to the point where their whole figure had thinned to the bones.

When that person was awakened by the nurse, they turned their head over slightly and Ye Qin's eyes widened as he

saw that face.

He had no idea that Cheng Xin had already deteriorated to this point after not even half a year.

Half a year ago, Cheng Xin once paid him a visit.

At that time, she had already been transferred from S-City to the capital to get treatment. Perhaps she had calculated the timing. At the time, Cheng Feichi was working outside and Ye Qin had just come over from school, having been dismissed early. They ran into each other at the elevator doors.

Ye Qin welcomed her into the house as calmly as he could and was debating how he should respond to her to avoid difficulties, when Cheng Xin spoke out.

"Are you two married?"

Ye Qin froze for a moment, then answered truthfully, "No."

Hearing this, Cheng Xin put on an understanding look. "In the end, he cares more about me, his mother, than you."

Whatever they chatted about after wasn't important. He wasn't sure how he sent her off, either. After she had left and the tea had cooled, Ye Qin sat by himself in the house for a while, holding the short solo script that he would be tested on in class tomorrow, unable to read it for the life of him.

It wasn't until Cheng Feichi returned in the evening that he changed his posture, pretending that nothing had happened.

Afterwards, Cheng Feichi still heard about this affair indirectly from the caretaker and asked Ye Qin later whether he'd heard anything unpleasant. Ye Qin shook his head like a pellet drum, insisting that he hadn't, saying that Cheng Xin had only come to check on how they were living. Seeing that he was more or less acting naturally, Cheng Feichi didn't ask further.

With regards to obtaining marriage licenses, neither of them took the initiative to bring it up in their day to day. For this kind

of thing, Ye Qin was used to having Cheng Feichi call the shots. If Cheng Feichi didn't bring it up, he also wouldn't think of it. They already lived together and wore rings. The license was but a piece of paper. To him, it wasn't that important.

But for the next few months after Cheng Xin's visit, the word "marriage" kept popping up in Ye Qin's mind: when he passed by the Civil Affairs Bureau, when he saw the male and female leads taking wedding photos during a shoot, and when he received a wedding invite from Zhou Feng and Liao Yifang.

Although it wasn't a big affair, just a gathering of several friends, when Ye Qin saw their marriage certificate, he got a feeling of fervent envy for the first time. These few days, after taking out the steel-plate and staying in the hospital with nothing to do, his mind started to wander off, putting him in a jittery mood.

Now, seeing Cheng Xin lying on the hospital bed on her last breath, Ye Qin suddenly felt ashamed. Cheng Feichi was so busy, but still had to take care of two people. He was already tired enough. Ye Qin shouldn't make more trouble for him.

He went back to his hospital room and opened a video chat with Cheng Feichi. Cheng Feichi was hurrying off to a dinner party that he hadn't been able to get out of. He apologized solemnly for being too busy to spend time with him these past few days, and told him that when he got the time, he would take him out to have fun.

Ye Qin simply didn't know what to say to make him not care so much about his feelings. After hanging up the video chat, he spaced out at the ceiling for a good while. After regaining his senses, he called Zhou Feng.

"You and the straight-A student's mom are staying at the same hospital? Then by all means, you should pay her a visit. That's your mother-in-law."

Ye Qin worried, "But I have a pretty poor relationship with

her, like the kind with cannons smoking and daggers pointed as soon as we see each other... What if she sees me, gets angry, and harms her health?"

"Didn't you say she's seriously ill and can't even open her eyes?" Zhou Feng suggested, "Take a secret peek, drop off some stuff, and leave. Just to let her know that you went to visit."

Ye Qin thought that this was doable. The next day, he ordered flowers and fruit online and made Zhou Feng pick a few boxes of supplements and send them over. That afternoon, he put on a jacket and carried bags of various sizes to the hospital building next door for a visit.

The gears in his brain went clickity-clack. The inpatient ward was most peaceful at this hour. The nurses were busy switching shifts, and the patients were all resting. He might even be able to not meet Cheng Xin face-to-face.

Unexpectedly, when he pushed the door open and looked in, the ventilating machine had been taken away some time ago, and Cheng Xin was leaning against the headboard, reading a book. When she heard movement in the doorway, she lifted her head and looked over, coming face-to-face with Ye Qin.

Ye Qin blanked out, standing in the doorway, unable to go in and unable to retreat. In contrast, Cheng Xin glanced at the things in his hands and adopted a welcoming posture. "Come in."

For the first half hour, no one said a word. Cheng Xin continued reading the book. Unable to sit still, Ye Qin took an apple to wash and peel.

He wasn't good at this. A perfectly fine apple was peeled into such a lump that he couldn't bear to look at it any longer, and he tossed it onto a plate. He washed two new apples and put them by the bedside.

Perhaps it was because Zhou Feng had raised those three words on the phone last night, but Ye Qin inexplicably felt that

the current situation strongly resembled a mother-in-law setting down rules. Subconsciously, he didn't dare to get angry and kept his waist straight as a pole, waiting for his elder's preaching.

After a few more minutes, Cheng Xin closed the book. Her breaths were as wispy as a cobweb and her voice was sapped of strength, yet the words that left her mouth remained overbearing. "Did you come today to check when I'll be dying?"

Ye Qin's heart jumped. He was mindful that she was a patient and desperately made himself look calm. "No. You're my elder. I just came to visit you."

Cheng Xin sneered in a manner that was both miserable and forced. She said, "You all want to see me die. I know."

Ye Qin realized the present Cheng Xin was different from before. Not only was she less aggressive and holding back her verbal jabs, but she showed a full-body fatigue towards life. It was as if, even if the best things in the world were placed in front of her, she would be unwilling to reach out and grab them.

Thus, Ye Qin had to weigh his words all the more, afraid to say something inappropriate and hurt such a frail woman even more.

Even so, he still held onto his contrary view. "No. At least not Cheng Feichi." He so rarely called Cheng Feichi by his whole name; he felt awkward and paused for a short moment, before adjusting his tone and continuing, "You're his mother and you're ill. He's the most affected of us all."

Astonishment seemed to flash across Cheng Xin's eyes. Then, she closed them, leaned her neck on the cushion, and turned to face the window.

This posture was clearly asking him to show himself out. Ye Qin stood up, thought for a bit, and decided to finish what he had to say.

"Actually, you know all that. You just don't want to admit

it. He would rather hurt himself than hurt you. That's enough to prove how big of a place you have in his heart. I hope you take care of your health, if only for the sake of how hard he worked over these past few years...if only just to stop us from being together."

Dreams were ultimately just wishful thinking. Fate never gives anyone an extra chance.

Cheng Xin couldn't survive the winter, and passed away on a foggy morning.

The funeral was organized singlehandedly by Cheng Feichi. Yi Zheng only showed up on the afternoon of the next day, purely because he wanted to hide from the Cheng family. Who knew that Cheng Feichi's maternal grandfather and grandmother would stay in the mourning hall for the entire night. When they saw him, they rushed over to hit him and shouting at him, "Give me back my daughter!" After a short scuffle, they suddenly gave up in, dejected. They helplessly buried their faces in their hands and wept.

They knew it was no use. Now matter how much they fought, their daughter could never come back.

When Cheng Feichi finished comforting the two elders and sent them home, two days had already passed. Ye Qin declined work early on and waited for him at home. As soon as he saw him, he stuck to him, asking if he wanted to eat or drink tea, if he was sore or if his leg hurt and he needed to sit and get a massage.

"No." Cheng Feichi turned down everything. He took off his black outfit, his face showing no other emotion except weariness. "Have dinner by yourself today. I want to sleep for a bit."

Because he was a public figure, Ye Qin didn't go to the funeral. Feeling that he couldn't offer any help, he could only put his efforts elsewhere. He bought groceries and made soup and even prepared a belly of comforting words to make his gege

not so sad. In the end, they weren't put to use. Cheng Feichi didn't want to eat. He didn't look like he had taken this very hard, and he didn't need Ye Qin's comfort.

Ye Qin half-heartedly had a few bites. Originally, he planned to go sleep in the room next door after finishing showering so as to not disturb Cheng Feichi's rest. Helplessly, he turned back and forth, unable to fall asleep, heart beating *thump-thump* and feeling restless. In the middle of the night, he tiptoed back to the master bedroom, lifted the covers, and crawled into bed. He gently circled his arm around Cheng Feichi's waist as he laid on his side in a posture full of possessive protectiveness. Only then did he fall asleep.

The next day, when Cheng Feichi woke up, he was locked in place by an arm and a leg.

Turning over, he woke up the person sleeping next to him. Before Ye Qin's eyes fully opened, he first grabbed onto Cheng Feichi's arm, asking anxiously, "Where are you going?"

Cheng Feichi said, "The washroom."

Ye Qin reluctantly let go and got out of bed with him.

When Cheng Feichi came out of the washroom, Ye Qin was still hanging at the door like a Door God, so tired that his head wobbled left and right, almost bumping against the wall.

Maybe it was because he'd been tired out of his mind for the past few days that relaxing suddenly made Cheng Feichi feel at a loss. He still had no appetite and wanted to go back to the room to rest after finishing a bowl of congee.

Ye Qin said, "I also didn't get enough rest. I want to sleep some more." After sitting together on the bed with Cheng Feichi, he took out a picture book from underneath the pillow and read it aloud like a bedtime story.

Cheng Feichi loved to read books. Sometimes, at night, Ye

Qin would read with him.

In order to not fall asleep while reading, Ye Qin specifically bought a pile of picture books with outstanding illustrations and lettering to put on the bookshelf. They were put together with Cheng Feichi's stack of professional books, adding much brightness to the gloomy bookshelf.

Today he took one called *The Giving Tree*. There was a green tree illustrated on the cover, and the inside pages had simple black and white illustrations paired with simple words. After reading a few pages, Ye Qin felt off. He closed the book, about to swap for a new one when Cheng Feichi stopped him.

"I'll read," he said. "You lie down and listen."

As soon as Ye Qin's head hit the pillow, he felt sleepy. At first, he still gave hums from time to time. As Cheng Feichi read on, he gradually stopped making noise. Very soon, other than a deliberately lowered reading voice, there was only the sound of slow, steady breathing.

After he finished and closed the book, Cheng Feichi saw "3-6-year-old children's book" written on the back cover and put the book down exasperatedly.

Turning to pull the covers over Ye Qin, Cheng Feichi found that his eyes were red, and that there was a teardrop that had yet to dry beaded on his eyelashes.

When he woke up again, it was already noon. This time he was woken by a strange movement in his palm.

Cheng Feichi rolled his eyeballs down to look at Ye Qin's fluffy scalp, lying on his chest. He felt soft lips pressing lightly against the scar on his palm, a little itchy and a little warm.

When he got up and changed his clothes, Cheng Feichi still debated if there was a need to explain things again to Ye Qin and let him know that this wound had nothing to do with him. As

soon as he opened the door and went out, he saw Ye Qin circling between the kitchen and living room like a little bee. Shortly, he brought out a table-full of dishes. The bowls and chopsticks were already set, and they could start dinner any time.

Ye Qin had just sat down when he fiercely slapped his forehead. "We can't eat non-vegetarian dishes right now, can we? I-I-I'll take it away immediately. Just pretend you didn't see."

Then he stood up, about to take them when Cheng Feichi grabbed his wrist and said, "Leave it. You don't have to take them away."

This meal was exceptionally peaceful.

Ye Qin was annoyed at himself for his clumsy words, always bringing up sore spots, and thought it best that he talk less. Meanwhile, Cheng Feichi was focused on tasting, very generously giving face to the head chef, not even wrinkling his eyebrows once.

After finishing, Ye Qin went to peel an apple. Because his skill was poor, fruit peels went flying all around even when he used the peeler. He squatted in front of the garbage bin, held his breath, and concentrated. He was more focused on an apple than college entrance examination papers, to the extent that when Cheng Feichi spoke, he didn't hear clearly for a while.

"Sorry?" he leaned his ear over and asked.

In the living room less than five meters away from him, Cheng Feichi said calmly, "Let's get married."

Ye Qin's hand shook, shaving off a huge chunk of apple.

He picked up the fallen apple peels on the floor and threw them in the garbage bin, still not daring to turn back and look at Cheng Feichi's expression.

Throat trembling continuously, Ye Qin tried his best to keep himself under control. He merely nodded and said in a manner that couldn't be more normal, "Oh, okay."

The two of them couldn't really be said to be "average" in their respective fields in the true sense of the word. Naturally, an affair as big as marriage couldn't be carried out spontaneously. They had to call Ye Qin's manager.

After finishing listening to them, Zheng Yueyue fell into silence for half a minute. The first question she asked was, "Private or public wedding?"

"He said he'll listen to me." Ye Qin ventured, "If I want a public wedding, Yueyue-jie, will you agree?"

Zheng Yueyue unexpectedly didn't reject it straight out. "If that's what you want, it's doable."

Since his admission to the capital's theatre academy, he had turned down a fair share of film offers; trying not to miss a single specialized course. Thus, he changed many strangers' innate assumptions of him being just a pretty face. This year, he took on two dramas, and although he didn't get leading roles, they were still serious dramas with famous directors, and added to the show that had already broadcasted. Ye Qin's acting in these dramas received no lack of good reviews, and he was on the path of transforming from an idol to a skilled actor.

Moreover, getting married officially was always better than rumors of keeping an illicit lover, so Zheng Yueyue thought that there was room to discuss a public wedding. However, they had to find a good time. They couldn't do it now.

Ye Qin was already very happy receiving this kind of answer. To him, as long as there was a possibility, he could work hard and overcome the obstacles. Immediately, he jumped about, and gave Yueyue-jie a kiss.

The day before getting their certificate, Ye Qin thought a bit and wound up visiting the prison in the east of the city after all.

"I'm getting married," he gave notice to Ye Jinxiang on the other side of the prison bars.

When he suddenly heard this news, Ye Jinxiang was far less calm than his son. He stood up from his chair, pressing, "With who? Which girl? How old is she? Where does she work?"

Ye Qin cared nothing for his delayed paternal love and said, "Not a girl. A man."

Ye Jinxiang fell silent for a while before asking, "Do I know him?"

"Yes," Ye Qin answered truthfully. "Cheng Feichi, my high school schoolmate from the adjacent class."

Ye Jinxiang gaped with a somewhat stunned expression. Then he slowly sat back with a smile mixed with regret and told Ye Qin, "You're no longer young. If you think it's good, then good. Your mom would think it's good, too."

He had originally wanted to anger this old man. Who knew that he would accept this so easily?

The next day, Ye Qin was wilted and spiritless, and understood on his own that it was because his childish attempt at provocation hadn't been satisfied.

When he reached the Bureau of Civil Affairs, he wore a face mask and followed Cheng Feichi, getting a number like everyone else.

Cheng Feichi was tall and had striking looks. Even standing at the back of the line, his presence was just as eye-catching as usual. Quite a few girls in front specifically turned around and looked at him. He didn't appear to be aware, standing in line looking to the front. Once in a while, he turned to ask Ye Qin whether he was tired and if he wanted to sit aside for a while.

There were a lot of people today and it looked like they had to wait a while for their turn. Cheng Feichi asked, "Are you thirsty? I'll buy you something to drink."

Ye Qin shook his head, his voice sounding muffled

through the mask. "I'm not thirsty or tired. You don't need to worry about me."

Cheng Feichi looked at him for a bit and said, "You're unhappy."

It was a statement, not a question.

Ye Qin was scared. "No, how am I unhappy? I've waited for this day for a long time. How can I be unhappy?"

He didn't realize that the more he explained, the more apparent it was that he was hiding something. Cheng Feichi stared at him for a while and then said, "You're unhappy. You can tell me if there's a problem. We don't have to get married today. I won't force you."

Ye Qin had a fright at the words "we don't have to get married" and clutched at Cheng Feichi's hand hanging at his side, as if scared out of his wits that he would run off. "You're the one who proposed. If you don't want to get married now, I'll...I'll..."

After "I'll"-ing for an age without coming up with an ultimatum, Ye Qin's exposed eyes gradually reddened, looking extremely wronged.

The two of them found a coffee shop close to the Bureau of Civil Affairs and sat down face to face.

After hearing Ye Qin recount his worries, Cheng Feichi's first reaction was to laugh. "You thought that I mentioned marriage on impulse?"

Ye Qin's hands clamped his fingers intensely under the table as he asked with widened eyes, "D-didn't you?"

Cheng Feichi's smile faded away. He gently tapped his index finger on the table a few times, and said after some thought, "Rather than say no outright, why don't I tell you why I didn't bring up marriage earlier? The main reason is that

I don't know how much of an impact getting married would have on your career. I have to keep you away from trouble as much as possible, just like your manager."

Ye Qin's eyes widened even more. This was completely different from what he had thought. He thought it would be some other reason, like Cheng Feichi finally being able to marry without burden after parting with his mother.

Of course, he didn't dare say this, afraid that he would trigger Cheng Feichi's sad memories. In the days after Cheng Xin passed away, even if Cheng Feichi didn't show it, Ye Qin could still detect the frailness and vacancy hidden behind a strong facade.

Though he didn't say it aloud, that didn't mean that he didn't care. The mother he had been codependent on for so many years had passed away. How could he not suffer?

Ye Qin privately came up with excuses for him and convinced himself to accept them, but he couldn't let go of this hang-up in his heart. Marriage should have been sacred and pure, shouldn't contain any tricks—or, to be more precise, shouldn't come with other misgivings.

He felt very conflicted, both leaping in joy at Cheng Feichi's "impulse" and despondent at these completely predictable, by-the-book plans.

"Then...then why..." Ye Qin didn't know what he himself wanted to ask. He had too many questions that he wanted to ask and yet he was tongue-tied, desperate for Cheng Feichi to read his mind.

Cheng Feichi didn't know how to read minds. He only voiced a few of his thoughts. "At first, I thought that we don't need these formalities. Tattoos or a so-called certificate joining us in marriage, it's all the same."

He wasn't good at reading too deeply into his subconscious behavior and had to stop to think deeper. Then, he looked at

the still dazed Ye Qin and said, "But then I found out that just because I don't need it doesn't mean that you don't need it. If this can make you happy, I'm willing to do it."

The two of them reentered the Bureau of Civil Affairs. The girl at the front desk, in charge of handling registration, looked at the two holding hands and said with a smile, "Figured it out so soon? Why don't I give you five more minutes? In a moment, after your pictures are taken and the certificate is stamped, it'll be too late to back out."

Thinking of how they had almost reached the front desk when they walked away from the queue, Ye Qin was so embarrassed that he could die. He rushed to hide behind Cheng Feichi, mumbling in defense through his face mask, "We're not backing out...we just left for a cup of coffee a moment ago."

Taking the filled-out registration form to take pictures, when Ye Qin took off his mask, the nearby female staff member exclaimed, "Hey, isn't that—" Mid-shout, she held back her voice, raised a finger in a shush motion and whispered, "Don't worry, we follow rules of confidentiality. We won't let anyone else know."

Perhaps it was because he got recognized that Ye Qin suddenly felt a little nervous. He clearly went in and out of the film studio all year round and yet was unable to let loose in front of a camera, neck straightening vertically and smile extra stiff.

The photographer rarely saw a pair of newlywed husbands so attractive, and wanted from the bottom of his heart to give them a good picture. He told them this photo would be kept for the rest of their lives, and directed them to move their heads closer together, to smile a little more naturally.

But the more this happened, the more Ye Qin was unable to relax.

He took another deep breath and suddenly felt the hand

hanging on his side being held. Cheng Feichi moved closer to him and whispered in his ear, "Ye Xiaoruan, smile."

As he said that, his long fingers intertwined with Ye Qin's one by one, bringing the two hands together, the whorls of their fingers pressing against the backs of each other's hands so that, apart from warmth, they could even feel the speed of the blood flowing underneath the skin.

A gust of wind suddenly blew through Ye Qin's mind, blowing his thoughts back to the High School No. 6 grounds of that year, when their ten fingers had been secretly intertwined behind their backs while they had to stay calm for fear that someone would see.

Now there was no need. Body and heart, soul and form, all belonged to each other openly.

Taking a deep breath, Ye Qin made a wide grin at Cheng Feichi. He turned his head to face the camera and the photographer captured that exact scene.

In the photo that came out, one person looked calm, but his face was soft, and his eyes held laughter. The other tilted his head, leaning against the shoulder of the man beside him, smiling magnificently with eyes that seemed to contain the only spot of warm sunlight piercing through the clouds on an icy winter day.

In early summer of that year, they climbed up the mountain together to pay their respects.

Actually, Ye Qin didn't have anything to say. He told all of his thoughts to his mom in his head. This time, other than telling her that Ye Jinxiang would be released from prison in half a year, there was only the matter of introducing and letting her know of his husband.

"Mom, I don't know if you still remember. You answered his call before. Back then, he was in the next class over, the star of the

honors class. He had very high grades, got the scholarship every year, and even won the first prize for the Physics and Chemistry Olympiads. He went to school abroad, and when he came back, he became the chairman of a large company. He makes really great meals and knows how to fix cars. That time when my bicycle tire burst, it was him who helped me fix it."

Ye Qin had a bank of ten thousand sentences he could summon from to sing the praise of Cheng Feichi and almost couldn't stop himself.

Finally, he steered himself back to the point, introducing as concisely as possible, "His name is Cheng Feichi. 'Feichi' is from the saying that 'one is of no small aspirations.' He embodies his name."

Ye Qin lifted his ring and said, "But don't worry, mom. I bought his ring. Though I still live in his house right now, one day I'll buy a huge house for him to live in and support him as my stay-at-home partner, so you're also his husband's mother, not his wife's." After saying this, Ye Qin couldn't help but think of himself as childish. He slowly put down his hand while staring directly at the face of the tombstone. After pondering for a moment, he spoke from his heart, "He's amazing and he's also amazing to me. I did so many bad things and he never got angry at me. He even married me...so...so I'll also treat him well, treat him amazingly well. Mom, do you think that's good?"

As they climbed down the mountain, Ye Qin's mood was still in a slump.

"I think my mom is mad," Ye Qin mumbled halfway down. "When she was still here, I was immature. Now that I'm slightly more mature, she's not here anymore. She must be mad at me, mad that I didn't grow up sooner."

Cheng Feichi didn't know Luo Qiuling, so he couldn't make

an objective interpretation of this opinion. He only thought that Ye Qin was a bit stubbornly hung up over a small detail and asked, "Is this important?"

"Of course," said Ye Qin, raising his head and looking at him. "Mom is my one and only family in this world, no matter where she is."

At these words, he saw a trace of astonishment flash through Cheng Feichi's eyes. Before he could pinpoint the issue, he heard Cheng Feichi say tonelessly, "We're married now. I'm also your family."

Because he accidentally said the wrong words, for the rest of the walk down the mountain, Ye Qin didn't even dare to breathe heavily.

The more he pondered, the more he thought that the words he had just said without thinking were particularly stupid. He had just said that he was going to treat Cheng Feichi amazingly well, and right after, treated him like an outsider. Even Ye Qin would be angry in his shoes.

But he really just said it offhandedly. Before Cheng Feichi was his family, he was his husband. In Ye Qin's eyes, a husband takes great precedence before family. A moment ago, his mind got all twisted up for a moment and treated the two equally.

Cheng Feichi was indeed "angry," but his hand never once let go of Ye Qin's and even gripped his wrist tightly when they got to the potholes and steep slopes that Ye Qin was afraid of. From time to time, he turned back to check on Ye Qin, keeping him in the protection of his bubble at all times.

Ye Qin knew the use of showing just the right amount of weakness from the benefit he received back when he pretended to be feeble. He knew better that it wasn't scary to make mistakes. Admitting to one's mistakes and correcting them were the principles of a well-behaved child.

Thus, when they got home and closed the door, he leaped into Cheng Feichi's embrace. Arms circling his waist, he clung onto Cheng Feichi, refusing to budge.

"Gege, I was wrong. I didn't mean it like that. You know that I didn't mean it like that."

With this soft voice in his ears, even if Cheng Feichi was fired up in anger, that anger would have dissipated.

Besides, he wasn't angry in the first place, just a little glum.

He sighed gently, "We're married now…"

This time Ye Qin reacted very quickly, and scrambled to reply, "Yes, we're married now. You are my gege, and my family."

Cheng Feichi felt amused when he heard this hasty explanation. Suddenly, he got an urge to tease the man in his embrace. "And?"

"And?" Ye Qin raised his head to look at him, blinking blankly. He got a thought that made his face break out into a flush and quickly buried his face again, mumbling incoherently.

Cheng Feichi grew curious at his shy appearance and urged, "And what else?"

"And…and…h-h…" Ye Qin's voice gradually lowered until only the first consonant of the last word was clearly pronounced and the rest of the answer became mumbled.

Almost brought to laughter by him, Cheng Feichi raised his hands and returned the embrace, locking him tightly in. He lowered his head and gently touched his lips to Ye Qin's heated, flushed earlobe.

"Little dummy."

Ye Qin *was* a little dummy. He believed everything Cheng Feichi said.

However, if he really looked into it, Cheng Feichi felt that the real reason that propelled him to bring up marriage half a year ago could be called an impulse. It was completely against his

normal habit of preparing for everything first and then acting.

When Cheng Xin passed away, a chunk of his heart had been dug out, and nothing could fill this empty space. Perhaps that was the feeling of losing a loved one that made him feel numb, empty, and at a complete loss.

He saw and kept an impression of everything that Ye Qin did for him, but at that time, he couldn't even take care of himself. Maintaining reason and not losing control in front of Ye Qin was already his limit.

Until he saw Ye Qin's tears.

The picture book story symbolized a mother's selfless sacrifice. After Cheng Feichi finished reading, he wasn't particularly touched. Everything Cheng Xin gave him served a purpose and needed to be repaid. But Ye Qin was different. His mother was warm and kind-hearted. She must have given the very best to her one and only child, just like in that book.

At that time, Cheng Feichi thought that he was still in this state, but when Ye Qin's mother passed away, how difficult it must have been for him, having no one by his side.

When he brought up marriage, Cheng Feichi's thoughts were very simple—he would give him a home, a real home with family.

Thinking back on it now, when hadn't he wanted to give himself a home?

Ye Qin was still mumbling into his ear in dissatisfaction, "I'm not a dummy. I'm very smart... In my next drama I'll be playing a young professor with the same level of attractiveness and IQ."

"You're not trying to pursue anyone anymore?"

"I still have to... It's just acting. It's fake. It's all fake."

Only you are real. Ye Qin swallowed these words back into his stomach, too embarrassed to say them.

But Cheng Feichi seemed to understand, lips curving into

a smile and landing kiss after light kiss on Ye Qin's outer ear, cheek, nose and lips.

They were familiarly warm and controlled, a light touch before parting. Kissed to contentment, Ye Qin hadn't had enough. He pursed his lips, moving closer in search for more kisses. Absolutely loving his cat-like behavior of running hot and cold, Cheng Feichi leaned over and pressed him down.

After a long time of inseparable grinding, the two of them broke apart. Cheng Feichi slipped his arms around Ye Qin's waist. Ye Qin circled his around his neck as his eyes fell on his face. He looked hazy and disorderly when in fact, he was focused and on fire with wavering eyes that brimmed with blatant infatuation.

Ye Qin licked his lips and said in between erratic pants that had yet to die down, "Gege...I love you."

As twilight fell through the window, Cheng Feichi almost sucked in by these bright, clear eyes.

It was only when he took Ye Qin back into his embrace that he realized his worries were foolish and unnecessary. He had already lost himself for a long time, lost himself in this pure love, indulged in its sweetness in spite of hardships.

The glimmer of the sunset, warm breaths, solid heartbeats surrounded the two of them most intimately.

Chen Feichi leaned his head down to kiss Ye Qin's soft temples. He closed his eyes and whispered into his ears, "I love you too."

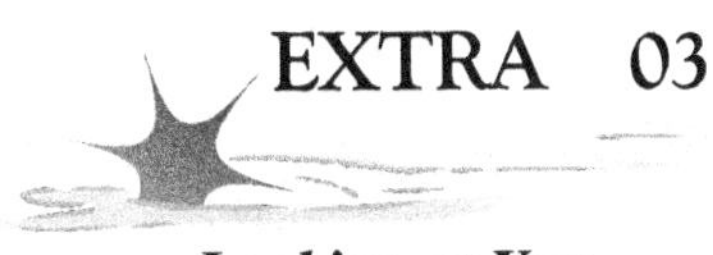

EXTRA 03

Looking at You

1.

During vacation, Ye Qin took a role on a variety show.

Before starring, he had already heard that this show was merciless to its guest stars regarding the format of the program and structure of the segments. They really worked those jobs on the streets in person, like scrubbing toilets and cleaning washrooms; no matter how dirty or tiring it was, they couldn't use a double. Risking their own safety for challenges was real; faced with a 10,000-meter-steep cliff, they had no choice but to jump. Wilderness survival was also real; if they gave you a straw hut, don't even think about sleeping in a tent. The charade of putting on appearances, posing for a picture, and then turning off the camera and immediately going back to sleep in a five-star hotel that happened in other shows was completely prohibited.

It was also precisely because of this raw reality that the ratings constantly stayed high. After broadcasting for two years, the program was already on its third season and its momentum had not only not declined, but shot up. It could be deemed a national phenomenon. Actors who were promoting movies and TV shows and singers who were releasing records were all dying for a chance

to get on the show just for the few seconds of publicity in the introduction segment.

Ye Qin got on the show this time by riding on the momentum of an on-the-road movie. In it, he played the third male side character whose part was more or less the same as the second male side character. The male protagonist was a top trender who, on the surface, said that he wouldn't go because he couldn't empty a slot in his schedule. In reality, everyone knew that the reason he didn't come was because he thought this show was too hard. When they couldn't get enough people, the director gave the opportunity to Ye Qin as a favor.

In truth, Ye Qin didn't want to go either, but Zheng Yueyue used all kinds of persuasion. Being frugal, he ended up compromising after seeing the guest star payment.

Afraid that he would encounter difficult situations while shooting the program, Ye Qin started to prepare a few days in advance, carefully reviewing past segments. Not only did he get a complete idea of the formula, but he even used his imagination to create many possible scenarios and dragged Cheng Feichi along to help him practice.

Today's setup was to borrow a vehicle from a stranger in public midway through a mission. Ye Qin only had four wheelers at home, so he went outside to borrow from a bikeshare and made Cheng Feichi push it to the neighborhood entrance, then pretend to be a stranger.

With everything ready, who knew that when Ye Qin saw Cheng Feichi riding the bike towards him from far away, he instantly forgot all of his mentally prepared script. He ran up to meet him, all four limbs about to climb onto the back seat of his bicycle.

Cheng Feichi reached out a hand, stopping him. "Excuse me, what are you doing?"

He was already in the role.

Ye Qin could only force himself to enter the scene, loosening his grip on the bicycle's back seat and saying politely, "Hello, I'm on a mission and wanted to borrow your bike."

He thought that it would go very smoothly with one of his own. Unexpectedly, Cheng Feichi didn't go easy on him one bit. He held up his wrist, looked at the time, and replied coldly, "Sorry, I'm in a rush. I can't lend it."

Ye Qin raised a sad finger. "I just need it for a little while. A little while, okay?"

Cheng Feichi propped one foot on the ground and looked at him amusedly. "How long is a little while?"

"Just...just half an hour."

"That's too long," said Cheng Feichi, shaking his head. "I still need to pick someone up."

"Who?"

Cheng Feichi glanced at him and said with an unchanged expression, "My wife."

He was completely serious. Meanwhile, Ye Qin's face flushed red in one motion. "I-I'll help you pick up your wife later."

Cheng Feichi laughed, "No, I have to go in person, or he'll get mad."

"He won't. He's not that petty of a person," Ye Qin said with extremely little confidence.

"It's not a matter of being petty or not," said Cheng Feichi. "I have to fulfill my promises to him."

Ye Qin frowned, about to cry. "Can't I give you my four-wheeler and you lend me your two-wheeler?"

Cheng Feichi raised an eyebrow and declined sternly, "No, my wife loves to ride on the back of my bicycle."

"...He doesn't have to."

"He has to."

Seeing that Ye Qin had no solution, Cheng Feichi suggested, "Why don't you help me ask him?"

A proper "act" turned into the passerby completely leading the guest star by the nose. Angry and embarrassed, Ye Qin yelled "Stop!" and flung his arms, giving up. He grumbled, "What kind of stranger's this hard to talk to?!"

Cheng Feichi broke from his role and returned to his normal state, releasing the handlebars and sitting upright. "Didn't you want me to give you as much trouble as possible?"

Thinking of those few "wife"s just now, Ye Qin's face burned hotter. "I-I didn't mean this kind of difficulty! Normal people wouldn't react like this..."

Cheng Feichi's eyes concentrated with laughter, and he purposely put his hands back on the handlebars. "Then let's do it again?"

This time, Ye Qin reacted quickly. He hopped onto the back of the bike, wrapping his hands around Chen Feichi's waist, and pressing his head to his back. "No, no," he urged, "you already picked up the person. Time to hurry home."

Cheng Feichi had work on the day of the shooting. Ye Qin rode the nanny van over, still flipping through the notes he'd taken a few days ago enroute.

Who would have thought that none of what was prepared ended up being used. The mission this time wasn't camping or drinking pepper spray or parachuting or some bizarre tasks on the streets. First thing in the morning, the host dragged the guest stars in a six-seat commercial vehicle to the back door of some amusement park in the suburbs. The host told them to sneak in without disturbing the guests, and then work inside to earn enough money for that night's accommodations.

More confusing than this mission was that Ye Qin was put

on the same team as "special guest star" He Hansong.

He Hansong came on the show on behalf of another drama about to screen. The director knew that the two were previous teammates and made the call to put them together. Other guest stars joked, "You two have known each other for so many years, so you must have a deep connection," and Ye Qin could only agree sarcastically.

People came and went in the amusement park. Having to consider keeping their characters hidden and finding an easy way to earn money, the scope of choices became very small.

After giving the female lead the opportunity of working at the small food stall, Ye Qin deliberately moved away from He Hansong. The two went one after another into the haunted house that no one would choose.

Ye Qin wasn't afraid of ghosts, but he was afraid of the dark. All along the way, he checked with the staff member to make sure he wouldn't be left alone inside, which wasted some time. After going into the changing room, they only managed to get their hands on a black cloak for him to dress up as a jiangshi.

"There was also a vampire outfit, but that was taken by Mr. He, who said he wanted to change outfits," the staff member there said.

Ye Qin just knew that no matter what, he couldn't stop He Hansong from setting up scheming up dirty tricks. Resigned, he put on the black robe and let the make-up artist deck out his face.

At the time he didn't think anything of it, but one glance at the mirror after putting make-up on and he almost fell apart. His entire face, from his forehead to his chin, was caked with a layer of thick white powder. Only the area around his eyes was left with two big holes, like black lumps. His original features were completely indistinguishable. Just moving his facial muscles felt like his skin was being stretched to the point where it hurt.

When Cheng Feichi sent a request for a video call, Ye Qin couldn't fully cover his face, so he covered the camera, not letting him see. "Don't pick me up today. I'll go back on my own."

"What happened?" Cheng Feichi stared at the complete darkness on the screen and asked suspiciously, "Is the wrap-up delayed again?"

"No, no." Ye Qin didn't need to lie about these matters and said honestly, "It's just, today's look is a bit strange... I don't want to show you."

When he heard this, Cheng Feichi knitted his eyebrows together, put down the pen in his hand and looked seriously at the screen. "What's going on? Was this planned by the program staff?"

No one knew better than Cheng Feichi how much Ye Qin cherished his own looks. Before, he had to prepare and clean up carefully just to go out for a date. After becoming an actor, he paid even closer attention to his image. If he stayed up all night shooting a scene and got dark circles, he never forgot to wear sunglasses to hide his face to prevent fans from taking a picture of them.

It wasn't necessarily the burden of being an idol. This was the etiquette of conduct towards others that Ye Qin absorbed from his deceased mother, not to mention the fact that he was born with a silver spoon and grew up pampered. In the past few years, he'd experienced hardships he'd never before encountered and things he'd never before known. So when he came across this kind of thing, he couldn't help but feel aggrieved.

After explaining, Ye Qin felt that he was making a mountain of a molehill. He blocked the camera with one hand. The other hand, which had nowhere to go, scrunched up the wide hem of the robe as he muttered, "It's my fault for coming late. I thought this place was very dark. You know I'm afraid of the dark. If I accidentally scare them..."

Cheng Feichi more or less got the gist from his incoherent

mumblings. Even if Ye Qin said several times that it was no big deal, he still decided to pick him up.

"Stay right there," Cheng Feichi said. "Wait for me."

2.

After hanging up the video chat, Ye Qin took a deep breath and fixed his mental state, resolving to do what was necessary.

He thought that this "wait" would take at least seven or eight hours. In the video, Cheng Feichi was clearly busy at work and wouldn't be able to leave for a while.

Not to mention that Cheng Feichi was low-key and didn't like showing his face to others. He had come to pick up Ye Qin several times before, and no matter how late it was, he'd always waited in the car. Sometimes the shooting got delayed until Ye Qin told him to go wait in the resting lounge, but he still didn't go in, just carried a laptop in the car in the glorified name of "finding extra time to work."

And so, Ye Qin took his ugly face and began to shoot the program.

At first, he was still a little upset, but as he was filmed, he let it go, especially when He Hansong, putting on an appearance very close to his usual look, was quickly recognized by passersby and eliminated. On the other hand, because of his terrifying look, people rarely spared him a second glance and he was able to muddle through to the second half. This ugly face unexpectedly became an advantage.

During the midway resting interval, the moving camera operator encouraged him, "Great job, Ye-ge! I just asked around and we're already in the lead!"

Ye Qin didn't know whether to be happy or not. He pointed at his own rigid, strained face. "Add some more powder, quick. It won't be scary if it falls off later."

Actually, it wasn't that scary in the first place. Ye Qin's place was at the end of the haunted house, behind a rock garden, where he was in charge of suddenly jumping out and giving guests a "surprise." But because his make-up was too dramatic and his jumping form was weird, he not only didn't scare anyone, but even made a few children laugh.

Pulled into another group photo by a fearless little boy, Ye Qin lifelessly made a victory hand. Then, in accordance with the kid's requests, he reached out both arms and jiangshi-hopped in a circle. He could already picture what kind of lively sight the bullet comments would be once the program aired.

As he was stuck between laughing and crying, the moving camera operator continued to fan the flames beside him, saying that their team had a chance to win. Even knowing that this was scripted, Ye Qin was still hyped up with a desire to win. He didn't eat lunch, just grabbed two bars of chocolate, and stuffed them in his pocket. He hid behind the rockery and secretly took a bite whenever there weren't many people around, sating his hunger and, at the same time, replenishing the necessary energy to play a ghost.

Since he ate secretly, he couldn't let anyone find out. Thus, when someone tapped Ye Qin's shoulder from behind, his first reaction was to run.

There was very little space in the haunted house. Besides him and the cameraman, there was no room left for a third person behind the rockery. Completely focused on running, Ye Qin didn't hold up his robes. A few steps later, he tripped on the robe and his arm was grabbed by the person behind him, pulling him onto his feet. He still wanted to flee until he heard that person speak.

"It's me."

The familiar, deep voice made Ye Qin shiver. He wanted even more to run, but since he couldn't, he first covered his face

with both hands. "Don't look! Don't look! I'm not Ye Qin!"

Cheng Feichi looked at the ring on his left ring finger and said, not knowing whether to laugh or cry, "Okay, okay. You're not Ye Qin."

During lunchtime, the haunted house was nearly empty. After struggling in the same spot for some time, Ye Qin still wouldn't show his face and asked uneasily in the eerie music, "How did you get here so fast?"

Cheng Feichi said, "I told you over the phone."

Ye Qin was going to cry. How did he know that "wait for me" equaled "I'll be there immediately"? How could he let Cheng Feichi see his ugly appearance?

"So, uh...I still need to film for a while," Ye Qin said bashfully, turning his body and hiding as much as he could. "Why don't you wait for me in the car?"

Cheng Feichi took a step forward and Ye Qin took two steps back, all the way to the wall.

Afraid that he would fall again, as he didn't look at his feet, Cheng Feichi was forced to stand still. He said helplessly, "That's it? You don't have anything else to say to me?"

"Huh?" Ye Qin raised his head. The hands covering his face opened up two slits that revealed shiny, black eyes. "Th-that's it. What else is there?"

The afternoon shoot lasted more than three hours.

When it was time to wrap up, Ye Qin shrank into himself and tried to erase his presence, afraid to alert the enemy. Who knew that, as soon as he pushed open the door, he saw a tall man stand in the doorway.

Cheng Feichi came in a hurry. He hadn't even changed out of his suit, just draped a coat over it. Now, seeing Ye Qin still wearing a thin costume, he immediately took off his coat,

draped it on Ye Qin, and pulled him into the chair in front of the make-up mirror.

For a while, Ye Qin blanked out. He wailed at the image of him in the mirror and covered his face with his hands. "W-w-why are you here?"

Cheng Feichi put the cup of hot water that had been prepared and sitting on the table into his hands. "Can't I be here?"

"No, no, just don't be here *right now...*"

Ye Qin was dying to put a basin over his head and pretend to be a shrunken turtle. Cheng Feichi leaned over to pry his hands off, but he refused to let go for the life of him. Cheng Feichi stopped insisting, straightened up, and said, "Then I'm leaving now."

He had just turned when the sleeve of his coat got caught directly.

Only half of Ye Qin's mouth showed, and his voice was smothered. "No, you can't leave."

3.

After getting a basin of hot water, Cheng Feichi held up Ye Qin's chin and slowly wiped his face with a wetted towel.

Ye Qin still refused to face reality. He couldn't cover up his face, so he closed his eyes in a typical example of burying his head in the sand—if he couldn't see, then others also couldn't see him.

Hot vapor rose from the soft towel, steaming Ye Qin until his nose tickled. He abruptly sneezed. Cheng Feichi grabbed a hot towel to wipe his nose and swiped its pointy tip after finishing.

Wrinkling his nose, Ye Qin hmphed, opening his eyes and about to flare up. When he saw the single-colored towel dyed with a whole mess of shades and colors, he thought of how much more of a colorful sight his face was. At once, he went speechless, shutting his eyes, lowering his head, and stewing in silence.

Cheng Feichi bent over in front of Ye Qin holding a towel, wiping a path down from his forehead. His other hand propped up the back of Ye Qin's head. When he reached a spot he couldn't wipe off, he rewetted the towel and repeated several times. His movements were gentle and filled with patience.

He even asked as he wiped, "Does it hurt?"

The powder caked on his face was slowly wiped off and the uncomfortably stretched stiff feeling also disappeared. Ye Qin bit his lip, shook his head, and said, "No."

He thought he covered it very well, yet he didn't know that Cheng Feichi could even feel the instant disarray of his breathing.

A large hand cupped over Ye Qin's trembling eyelids. The swirling, rising steaminess made their skin unable to separate. Cheng Feichi stopped beating around the bush and sighed softly, "If you were treated unfairly, you have to tell me."

Ye Qin jolted. "N-n-n-no. How can I be treated unfairly? Who's talking nonsense?"

For a moment, Cheng Feichi didn't know if he should laugh or what to do with this little liar. He curled his fingers and scratched the soft skin on Ye Qin's chin. Ye Qin shivered and tilted back his head to evade.

When he met that pair of deep eyes watching him, he couldn't maintain his resolve. Ye Qin slowly approached and took Cheng Feichi's hand in both of his, swinging it too and fro. He said softly, "Really, no one bullied me. You can't avoid these kinds of encounters in this industry. If everyone looked to their family for support for these things, wouldn't this industry be a mess?" As he said this, he patted his own face and said optimistically, "I was just ugly for a moment. After a while, no one will remember."

The word "family" lit a warm fire in Cheng Feichi's heart. Suddenly thinking of something, he curled up his lips and laughed.

Hearing this, Ye Qin raised his head and looked at him.

From Cheng Feichi's expression, he was also suddenly reminded of something. He immediately opened his eyes wide in a fierce pretense and struck first by saying, "Don't say it! You can't say it... or think of it!"

As a result, he was the first to crack, his cheeks deflating and huffing out a "ha." And then, with a colorful face that had yet to be fully cleaned off, he buried himself in Cheng Feichi, pressing, pressing his ear to his chest, and feeling it shake from laughter, smiling so hard his eyes squinted into two seams.

It was obvious what the two of them were thinking of.

Back in school, Ye Qin went around fussing and stirring up trouble all day long, always bragging that he was going to support Cheng Feichi. Once, Cheng Feichi had been moved to the very back of the class because he was tall and Ye Qin had rolled up his sleeves, saying that he was going to have a talk with the home-room teacher.

"Do you still remember putting a band-aid on me that day that I got hurt?" Ye Qin asked, hugging his waist.

Cheng Feichi said, "No."

Ye Qin lifted his head in surprise and looked at him. "You really don't remember?"

The laughter stayed in Cheng Feichi's eyes as he raised his hand and squeezed Ye Qin's cheek. "I only remember that this is very soft."

The same voice. The same tone. In a split second, a beautiful scene materialized in front of Ye Qin's eyes like a firework explosion. He was absentmindedly brought back to the quick and shallow first kiss in the back row of the dim classroom. It made his heart thump wildly and his breathing go shallow and heated.

At the same time, Ye Qin thought that the past left behind many regrets from unexpected turns of events.

That was why he couldn't no longer let the present slip by.

He grasped the hand that Cheng Feichi placed on his face, sliding it downwards as he said, "Th-th-then do you still remember me saying I also fell and hurt my butt?"

Cheng Feichi didn't speak. He just fixed his eyes on him and smiled, fully intending to listen and follow him.

"Then." Ye Qin got up and guided Cheng Feichi's hand behind him, lifting his wide robe and sticking it inside. He continued, stuttering even more heavily, "B-back then, I wanted to say, 'Gege, try here. Th-th-this is also very soft.'"

4.

After removing his makeup and changing clothes, Ye Qin left to tell the staff on-site that he was about to leave. The director called out to him, "Don't leave yet. We still have a set of photos to shoot."

It turned out that there was a reward for winning the game. Ye Qin let the female lead have the grand prize. The program staff felt very bad about making him wear ugly make-up for the whole day, and had the good foresight to realize that the fans wouldn't be satisfied either once this was broadcast. And so, they added a temporary reward: they shot a collection of cover photos using the street of the theme park as the backdrop, which had Republican-era theming.

At first, Ye Qin didn't want to shoot, but when the assistant shook out the clothes for him to have a look, he couldn't look away: a vest, a tie, and a fitted shirt that was ironed as flat as a board, and the material was very well-textured. How nice it would look on him.

Ye Qin was moved after wearing ugly robes for an entire day. He ran back to the resting lounge to discuss with Cheng Feichi, telling him that there was an additional shoot that needed him to stay for a while. Cheng Feichi agreed and told him he would wait

for him in the car.

Ye Qin cheerily put on the costume, tying the tie as he walked towards the shooting location.

He wasn't good at wearing anything that needed to be tied up, and couldn't figure out the tie for ages. Just as he became anxious enough to seek the assistant for help, a hand reached out from behind. Then, another arm rested on his shoulder, forming an embrace from behind. Long, slender fingers pinched on both ends of the tie and skillfully twisted it into a knot.

Upon seeing the ring on the ring finger of the person's left hand, Ye Qin knew who it was. He stared dead straight at the hand that helped him tie the tie and whispered, "Didn't you go to the car?"

Cheng Feichi tilted his head slightly, pressing his cheek against Ye Qin's ear. He said, "I want to see how you look while working."

Ye Qin had seen countless times the focused look Cheng Feichi had as he worked, but this was the first time he was being looked at in return.

The two of them returned together to the shooting location. All the staff members said hello and struck up small talk with Cheng Feichi, one after another. When it was time to take shots of Ye Qin, they knowingly let Cheng Feichi have the best viewing angle.

Ye Qin was much more nervous than him. He couldn't relax his expression and his movements were also a bit reserved.

For a set of photos of looking into the distance from underneath a tree, the photographer had him look directly at the audience seating area, in hopes that he could better elicit emotion. He blushed immediately and cast a glance at Cheng Feichi before looking away. As the shooting went on, he couldn't help but look

over, and his cute, shy, happy look was completely captured by the photographer.

Cheng Feichi also looked at him. They weren't close, but Ye Qin could feel the affectionate warmth flowing through his eyes.

That warmth wrapped around him impenetrably, acting as armor that protected him as well as a harbor that he relied on for anchorage. It made him fearless of the cold, the wind, and the rain henceforth. It made him unafraid of everything.

After wrapping up the shoot and returning to the resting lounge, he unexpectedly ran into He Hansong, who had yet to leave.

Ye Qin couldn't be bothered to waste words on him, keeping to himself as he took off his clothes and makeup. Cheng Feichi was still outside.

But He Hansong didn't plan on letting him off. He walked over, first dangling the clothes that he had just taken off and "tsk"-ing disdainfully, then crossing his arms and looking at Ye Qin through the mirror, ridiculing, "With the way you've made a habit of bringing along your patron and showing him off, are you scared other people don't know that you sold your ass to get promoted? Ride this one's coattails carefully. I hear that President Cheng's got a mess of a family. Perhaps someday, someday, his wife will come looking for you and crush your career in the entertainment circle with a single finger."

Ye Qin had heard enough of his mockery that he'd long learned how to let it enter through one ear and leave through the other. However, today he only felt incendiary, unrestrained anger.

He had no problem with someone wrongfully saying that he was being fed by a patron, as long as he himself had a clear conscience. But what had Cheng Feichi done wrong to get picked on along with him?

Ye Qin shot up and banged the bottle of makeup remover on the table at the same time, scaring out a tremble from He Hansong.

"Wife? *I* am the wife." Ye Qin lifted his chin and side-eyed He Hansong. He pointed at the doorway and then jabbed his own chest, proclaiming imposingly, "He is my lawful husband."

Then, he thought that what he said wasn't grandiose enough and tacked on two terms hot-bloodedly, "I am the primary spouse! The OG partner!"

5.

After leaving the set, the news of Ye Qin's marriage first spread through the tight-knit entertainment circle and then rapidly spread outward, and with some "thoughtful people" fanning the flames, it climbed onto the hot topic list for two hours.

"You brat. Just a few days ago, you said that you would 'completely follow my plans,' but it turns out that was all an act. Here I am pre-emptively sketching up the best way to go public and you just plan everything out for me. You've got some skills, you."

Faced with Zheng Yueyue's scolding, Ye Qin could only curl up, make himself look small, and apologize, leaning over saying with his hands covering the microphone, "Sorry, Yueyue-jie. It's my fault. I was an idiot... At the time, I got angry and didn't think too much..."

After agreeing on a solution, Ye Qin got another round of chewing out. He rubbed his ears and hung up the phone. Beside him, Cheng Feichi asked, "You got yelled at?"

Ye Qin pretended like it was nothing. "No. Isn't it almost New Year's? We were just chatting."

Cheng Feichi returned to work in the study and Ye Qin posted on Weibo following Zheng Yueyue's order. He felt a bit like shutting himself off from the outside. After posting,

he immediately logged off the account, afraid to look. Putting down his cellphone, he went to the kitchen to see what ingredients were left in the house and they were enough to make lunch.

Soon after, Cheng Feichi also went into the kitchen. "Shall we go see a movie this afternoon?"

Ye Qin shook his head over. "Nah, nah, let's not go out. It's the same watching at home."

Without making a sound, Cheng Feichi washed his hands. He then helped him scoop out the washed vegetables from the water, put them on the cutting board, and chopped.

There was another wave of silence. Ye Qin couldn't stand it yet again. He slowed down when picking out the vegetables and asked hesitantly, "When you said that I could go public at any time in any way, were you serious?"

Cheng Feichi's hands also paused as he replied, "Do you need me to cooperate?"

"No, no." Ye Qin denied hastily. "I just wanted to check... Just now, just ten minutes ago, I went public on Weibo."

Cheng Feichi nodded, understanding why Ye Qin didn't want to go out. He asked, "Did someone already yell at you?"

Seeing his calm reaction, Ye Qin also calmed down quite a bit and even got in a joking mood. "Yeah, she yelled at me so furiously. Will you get me another manager?"

Cheng Feichi's hands froze as he turned and looked at him. "If you want."

A little startled by his serious expression, Ye Qin hurriedly explained that he was just making a joke. Zheng Yueyue had stayed with him for so many years and did him countless favors, big and small. How could he burn this bridge and replace her on a whim?"

During the meal, Ye Qin, still having some reservations, asked Cheng Feichi if he was serious about what he said a moment

ago. Cheng Feichi said, "I'm serious if you are."

Ye Qin put on a withered face. "I didn't think He Hansong would really tell other people. I even thought that he would rein himself in once he knew about our relationship."

Cheng Feichi had yet to express his opinion on this. He handed Ye Qin a rib and asked, "Then, what about you? Are you happy?"

"Happy about what?"

"Are you happy that we're public?"

Ye Qin chewed on chopsticks and thought for a moment. Then he smiled widely and said, "Yeah."

They no longer had to hide. He could walk down the streets holding hands with Cheng Feichi. He could openly tell fans that the ring on his finger was a wedding ring. Of course he was happy.

Cheng Feichi nodded. "In the future, you have to tell me everything. Don't take risks by yourself."

And more importantly, don't suffer through grievances by yourself.

Ye Qin smiled ear-to-ear and agreed cheerfully. He lowered his head and dug into his rice for a bit when he suddenly had a thought. He lifted his head and winked, asking, "Then, are you happy?"

Cheng Feichi smiled in silence. Ye Qin threw a fit, demanding that he say it. He wasn't beyond threatening to go on a hunger strike, and Cheng Feichi, nagged until he was helpless, said, "As long as you're happy."

As long as you're happy, I'm happy.

6.

The hubbub surrounding actor Ye Qin's marriage dispersed after he posted an official acknowledgement on Weibo and things slowly calmed down.

He didn't count as a top trender. For the past two years, he had been deeply focused on honing his acting skills to transform into an acting powerhouse and hadn't generated a lot of discussion amongst the masses. Only that afternoon did his news reach the long-abandoned campus forum of the capital's High School No. 6 and gave rise to several hundred students following and commenting.

OP meticulously reposted the undeniable picture-proof sent out by marketing accounts, screenshots of Ye Qin's Weibo and the picture on it. Ye Qin opened the post and immediately relived everything.

The first picture was a sneak photo that had been circulated on the web for several days. In the photo, he was dressed in historical costume and make-up and was putting on a beret in the same color scheme as his armor. One foot was propped up on the curb for Cheng Feichi to stoop over and tie his shoelaces in a half squat.

The second picture was posted by Ye Qin himself. It was much clearer and evidently a normal photo. However, this picture didn't capture any faces. Two men stood side by side facing the sunset, looking far into the distance. The camera was set up from behind. The shorter man had a coat that didn't quite fit him draped over his shoulders and leaned into the taller man in a dress suit.

The only solid proof was the beret that was identical to the one in the sneak picture.

It could already be seen from the photo that the two of them were pressed together tightly, but other than the staff members who were there at the time, no one knew that apart from the photo, their hands were also held together tightly.

The discussion on the forum was quite civil, especially when someone reposted the Weibo message digging out the

true identity of Ye Qin's marriage partner. Everyone not only found out that Ye Qin was a fellow alumnus of High School No. 6 but that his partner was actually the former school hunk with Cheng for a last name, who had continued to stir up chaos in the forums for many years. In the collective glory of producing and of keeping the goods in the family, everyone expressed thankfulness.

But there were still dissenting voices that spread from within.

Comment 72: *[I never would have thought it was them!]*

Comment 81: *[Although quite relieved, I... still feel like I received a thousand tons of damage. School Hunk Cheng was my first love! My heartthrob!]*

Comment 85: *[Is it too late now to say that I don't agree to this marriage?]*

Comment 89: *[They couldn't have been together from when they were in school rite? After all this time, the whole sensation over a bunch of couples getting together was a cover for these two?!]*

Comment 90: *[yq practically ran amok in school. who knows if he forced cfc]*

Comment 93: *[r u an idiot, using so many abbreviations? Don't bring that stuff over from the fan circle. Who was running amok? Ye Qin was cute as heck and good to his friends, everyone knows this.]*

Comment 95: *[I found the truth.]*

Comment 97 re: 95: *[Insider? Don't leave! Tell us quickly!]*

Comment 101: *[I was in the science stream back then. I just remember Ye Qin visited our class all the time and looked super school-girly... turns out it was to get with Cheng Feichi.]*

Comment 105 re: 101: *[Omigod!! What did I miss back then!?!? Studying is harmful!!]*

Comment 101: *[Didn't someone post a picture of Cheng Feichi together with a girl last year?]*

Comment 113 re: 111: *[look at ur comment nbr, be careful of

ending up single... ur all too young, always guessing the girls.]

Comment 115: [**cry* are your blessings all real? Am I the only one jealous? Whys_the_green_eyed_monster_always_me.jpg]*

Comment 121: [*Lemme make it known that I had a crush on Cheng Feichi back then and even gave Ye Qin 2 love letters to pass on.]*

Comment 125 re: 121: [*u lost, sis. i gave him 8 *facepalm*]*

Comment 128 re: 121: [*My sympathies... who hasnt secretly given their heart over to cfc... now that u mention it, does anyone still rmbr that nameless girl who gave him breakfast?]*

Comment 136: [*no wonder... no wonder i always saw cheng feichi buy lollipops at the corner shop...]*

Comment 141: [*They've already been together for a long time, i ran into them kissing in the staircase after evening self-study]*

Comment 145 re: 141: [*sis dont leave! Pls describe the kiss in detail!]*

Comment 149 re: 141: [*So they were rly together for... ahhhhh first loves are so sweet!!]*

Comment 165: [*but didn't the Ye family go bankrupt? He didn't do well in the entertainment circle either. Cheng Feichi's family's so rich. Will they accept him?]*

Comment 167 re: 165: [*Probably pulled some tricks. So what if it's first love? How can it be so easy to become part of a rich elite family?]*

When Ye Qin saw this, he got mixed feelings and was about to make some comments using a mule when he saw a reply from an ID named "YiRanZiLe"—or, "pleased and happy." [*Coming off anon. I'm Comment 141, Ye Qin's classmate. They got together long ago and still love each other to this day, so, so sweet. It's ok to be jealous but no need to worry so excessively abt their affairs.]*

Someone replied very quickly: [*gurl, thanks for letting us know the truth. Some ppl in the thread r rly weird and can't bear*

to see others be happy. Altho... were you all crushing on Cheng Fei-chi back then? Was I the only one who liked Ye Qin?]

Comment 222: [Ya, Ye Qin's handsome and generous. All u jealous ppl never had him buy u fried dhicken have u?]

Comment 225 re: 222: [Mind ur words! Let's be civilized people. But now that you mention it, I remember when Cheng Fei-ichi got the Olympiad first prize, Ye Qin invited the entire science stream for bubble tea. Shit, this goddamn love!]

Comment 228: [Ye-tongxue, I was in the same class as you. We took part in the same sports competition together. Do the rich elite need drivers/attendants/handymen? Quick, look at me wav-ing my hands!]

Ye Qin choked and hurriedly scrolled past this section. An ID named "FREEZE UR ASS AND UR GRANDDAD'S ASS TOO" posted: [Do they need u to be concerned abt their sweet and loving and harmonious sex life? Pah!]

Following that was an ID named LiaoYifang01:

[Hi everyone, I was the science stream class (2)'s class moni-tor, see my ID for name.

The people who said that Ye-tongxue ran amok bossing ev-eryone around in the thread must have some misunderstanding about him. As his classmate, I can testify on my conscience that Ye-tongxue was kindhearted, diligent, and studious in school and Cheng-tongxue was mature, earnest, and outstanding. They are very compatible, have a very good relationship, and are worthy of receiving all your blessings.

Also, posts with vulgar language will be deleted by the mod-erator and the poster will be banned for 30 days. Everyone, please mind your manners, and speak and act cautiously.]

Ye Qin saw this and broke out in giggles. When he stopped, he quickly logged on and clicked the reply button. But then, he didn't know what to say. After blanking out for quite a while, he

entered the two words, "Thanks everyone," and clicked send.

7.

As evening fell, a newly registered Weibo side account gave Ye Qin's Weibo a thumbs up and then replied with a heart emoji that looked like the official.

A little later, the post in High School No. 6's forum that had already amassed over 500 comments welcomed a new participant. An ID named "cfc0215" replied to "YourbigbroQin_notQing"'s comment:

[Put your phone down and come out to have dinner.]

EXTRA 04

Sleeping Beauty

ONCE in a while, when the two of them were free, they would get groceries at the supermarket like normal couples.

Apart from eggs, Ye Qin was also very careful and selective about buying milk. A buy-one-box-get-three-packets-of-a-yogurt--drink over here, and a-buy-one-box-get-a-free-glass-bowl over there, could put him in a bind and make him hesitate over both.

Cheng Feichi saw Ye Qin poke a few times at the yogurt drink package. He had just decided to get this box when Ye Qin hastily threw out a "Wait for me!" and then took off without a trace.

He went to look at the prices of the yogurt drinks and glass bowls.

When he came back, he decidedly took the case of milk bundled with the glass bowl, still panting, "T-this bowl is more expensive. Better value."

Cheng Feichi took it and used his other hand to wipe off the sweat that dripped to the tip of his nose. He asked, "Did you run that far just to compare prices?"

Ye Qin covered his mouth weakly with his face mask and wrinkled his nose when he heard this. "Anything's better than nothing."

After coming back home and eating, Ye Qin took a shower and changed, making himself nice and fresh. He went into the bedroom and opened up the wardrobe, fiddling with his new clothes for the *n*th time.

There was a charity dinner during the Lunar New Year. Cheng Feichi ordered an expensive dinner suit for Ye Qin, who was attending as a guest.

Every night when Ye Qin got home, he took this dinner suit out of the wardrobe to admire and feel. He held it over himself in front of a mirror, angling back and forth, but could never once bring himself to try it on.

Cheng Feichi, who knew that he liked to show off his looks, told him to wear it to his heart's content. "If it gets dirty, I'll order a new one."

Ye Qin shook his head. "No, no. Usually there's no occasion for wearing a dinner suit. It'd be a waste."

Come to think of it, the Ye family was quite plentiful in assets once, despite not belonging to the rich and powerful. Ye Qin grew up pampered. Between all the expenses put into clothing to food to houses to transport, what good things had he not seen before? Now that he had fallen to a point where he had to carefully consider before buying a single piece of clothing, if others knew, they would certainly sigh at how fortunes rose and fell.

In no mood to lament, Cheng Feichi patted the edge of the bed. "Come here."

Ye Qin put away the dinner suit, walked over, and sat beside Cheng Feichi. He meekly took the hot milk Cheng Feichi handed him, took a sip. Narrowed his eyes, he exhaled in satisfaction, as comfortable as a kitten being stroked.

Cheng Feichi raised his hand to rub Ye Qin's fine, soft hair and pinched the skin on his nape in passing. "Did you put on

weight?"

Ye Qin, who depended on his looks for a living, first startled and then understood. Guiding Cheng Feichi's hand to his waist, he giggled, "Touch and see then, do I also need new pajamas?"

Even after being seen through, Cheng Feichi's face was as straight as always. He nodded and said, "Okay, I was going to buy a new pair anyways."

Before sleeping, Ye Qin browsed through couples' pajamas on Taobao for half an hour. Most were male and female sets, super uninteresting. Cheng Feichi sat beside him, holding a book and leaning against the headboard. Ye Qin threw down his cellphone and burrowed into his chest. He smelled the scent of body wash on him and yawned.

"If I really did gain weight, I can just wear your pajamas."

Cheng Feichi laughed, "You don't have a problem with someone else's old pajamas?"

Ye Qin, who used to always find a problem with this and that, shook his head. Rubbing his cheek against the warm chest, he mumbled, "Gege, you're not someone else."

On the day of the charity banquet, Cheng Feichi and Ye Qin went together.

Other than figures from the entertainment industry, many celebrities also came. Mr. Fang, the organizer, set up a common area outside of the venue for the guests to rest. Inside was gorgeous attire and soft laughter, just like a large social gathering.

As soon as he entered, Ye Qin ran into an acquaintance. Today, Liu Yuqing wore a bright yellow long dress that accentuated her elegant figure and graceful posture. Upon spotting Ye Qin, she smilingly handed him a drink. Upon seeing that he had someone with him, she feigned surprise and exclaimed, "So we could bring along a family member? Damn, let me hurry and

call over my own."

Ye Qin knew she was making fun of him and laughed, "With you and your husband both in the entertainment circle, what's the need to bring along the whole family for a free meal?"

Liu Yuqing made a face like she was getting away with an evil plan. "Oh, so President Cheng is taking advantage of you to get a free meal?"

Ye Qin immediately became flustered and embarrassed. He waved his hands repeatedly. "No, no, he also came on invitation." As he spoke, his big eyes fluttered and cast a glance both sincere and pitiful at the person beside him.

The "magnanimous" Cheng Feichi naturally wouldn't argue against him. The three of them found a place to sit and chat for a little while. Ye Qin got a call from his manager telling him that he had to pay a visit to his friends in the same group. Before leaving, he didn't forget to urge them to save his spot.

Liu Yuqing watched Ye Qin's figure walk off. She put down her cup. "President Cheng, how did you find time today to come to this sort of small occasion?"

Only when Ye Qin's figure completely disappeared did Cheng Feichi move his eyes back from the crowded doorway. "I came with him," he said curtly.

"Mutual first loves, belonging to each other wholly—it's practically a love story from a novel," sighed Liu Yuqing. "I'm so jealous."

Cheng Feichi laughed, "We were separated for a while in the middle."

Liu Yuqing expressed understanding as an experienced person. "Education and career are the two major obstacles in a relationship."

"It wasn't fully for objective reasons." As he said this, Cheng Feichi suddenly had a thought and asked, "You're Ye Qin's senior,

so maybe you know what his circumstances were when he first joined the entertainment circle?"

Ye Qin was pulled along by Song Xu into a half-hour chat.

The topic started on the performance at the venue and somehow weaved into personal affairs. Song Xu said that his girlfriend outside of the showbiz circle had gotten pregnant and he was debating whether to leave the industry.

Ye Qin was very surprised and also ashamed. Ever since he moved out of the shared dormitory, he very rarely went back. Aside from work, he stuck to Cheng Feichi all day long and didn't even report in at his own workplace as many times as he reported in at Cheng Feichi's. He paid even less attention to his junior Song Xu, to the point that now was his first time hearing of such important news.

He urged Song Xu to not reach a decision so easily. His acting career had just taken off at such a young age, it was too much of a pity to give up on it now. The best thing to do was to find a balance between career and family life as much as possible.

On the way back, Ye Qin mulled over it. Song Xu had just turned twenty. He was still a child, and yet he was already about to become a dad. Young people nowadays were truly wild and took no account for consequences.

Those two were still sitting and chatting on the corner sofa. As he approached, he heard Liu Yuqing's clear voice, "We're also getting ready to have a kid. When the time comes, we'll have you two be godfathers."

They were also discussing kids.

Ye Qin walked over and sat down. He asked what they were talking about, and Liu Yuqing secretively made a "shh" motion. She said, "We're about to enter the venue. Be careful not to let the surrounding reporters overhear."

The banquet lasted until 10 p.m.

After a long day, Ye Qin dozed off with his head leaning against the car window. Afraid he would get cold, Cheng Feichi lifted his head off the glass and put it on the back of the seat while waiting at a red light.

Ye Qin made a very small yawn, struggling to look at Cheng Feichi through half-shut eyes. "Gege, do you want...kids?"

At first, Cheng Feichi was startled, but soon after he understood. "Why ask this all of a sudden?"

Ye Qin smacked his lips a few times, so tired that the corners of his eyes moistened. "I just...just wanted to ask."

As Cheng Feichi had grown accustomed to this lil' guy's half-asleep ramblings long ago, he also answered in a half-truth, "I have a kid at home. One is enough."

Perhaps because he got the answer he wanted, that night Ye Qin slept super soundly.

The next day was the weekend. With no plans to leave the house, the two of them put on a movie to idle away the afternoon.

Ye Qin went to the bathroom in the middle. When he came out, he mischievously used his wet hands to flick water everywhere, like usual. Cheng Feichi caught him and put his wrists together, then used a tissue to carefully wipe along all the spaces in between his fingers until they were dry.

Ye Qin was ticklish all over. Just rubbing against his palm made him giggle. Wanting to move away but unable to break free, he laughed until he was out of breath and complained that Cheng Feichi was all brute force, just like a bison.

Seeing Ye Qin's wrists pinched until they showed circular red marks, Cheng Feichi used a little less force. "You're still a kid. Of course you're not as strong as me."

Ye Qin thought of the brainless question he asked in the car yesterday and blushed. Suddenly, he thought of a related past

event and probed, "Then do you remember when I fell from the high bar during gym glass in high school…"

Cheng Feichi nodded. "I remember."

"What were you thinking?" Ye Qin voiced the doubt in his heart. "I was so…so bad then. I didn't help you prove your innocence, and I even poked out the wheels of your bike. Why did you save me?"

Now that Ye Qin's hands were dry, Cheng Feichi threw away the tissue and wrapped Ye Qin's hands in his, massaging them. "I didn't think." He paused for a moment, then added, "If you fell, it'd hurt."

The two sentences, so simple that no hidden meaning could be found in them, startled Ye Qin.

Even though Ye Qin had given him so many unpleasant memories, Cheng Feichi never thought of retaliating. Moreover, from the past to the present, he was never willing to let Ye Qin suffer even a little bit of pain.

As if he knew Ye Qin loved to let his thoughts run wild, Cheng Feichi used actions to show candidly that, from start to finish, he his forgiveness and love had never diminished.

Even if taking belated action after things had changed with time held no meaning whatsoever, every time he realized this, an urgent feeling of guilt always surged in Ye Qin's heart. He felt that what he could give Cheng Feichi was too little.

What else could he do for him?

For the latter half of the movie, Ye Qin's head drifted into outer space. After skipping through countless programs that he thought were not sincere enough, a bold and unrestrained thought went madly shooting off the rails.

And so, Cheng Feichi returned from washing fruits in the kitchen to see Ye Qin sitting with legs folded on the sofa and using

his arm to make back-and-forth gestures at his waist.

He thought this little guy wanted to get a tattoo or something and was about to advise against it when he heard Ye Qin mumble, "Back then, if...five years had gone by...the kid would be this tall, right?"

Further inquiry revealed that the drama Ye Qin had recently been signed to had a "runaway mother pregnant with child" plot, nowadays popular with the crowd. Adding on how everyone had been constantly mentioning kids in front of him for the past few days, he thought that if reality could be as dramatized as drama series, then, when the winners had been announced back then...

The subject was quite inconceivable. Ye Qin stammered as he described it. Before he finished, Cheng Feichi smiled. "Then we'll try tonight."

Ye Qin also realized afterwards that this connection was beyond silly and held in laughter until his face turned red. He held up a body pillow to hide it and, still worried, asked again, "Are you sure you don't want kids?"

He had just thought that if Cheng Feichi wanted a kid, they could adopt one. Although he didn't like kids, if they could be good to his gege and make him happy, Ye Qin wouldn't mind sparing half of his attention.

"I don't." This time, Cheng Feichi refused resolutely. He took away the body pillow in front of Ye Qin and popped a washed strawberry into his mouth. "You are enough," he repeated plainly.

A chance to talk about those five years was hard to come by. Ye Qin pillowed his head on Cheng Feichi's lap and recounted the past amidst the soft music of the movie's end credits.

"Actually, I don't remember very clearly. Days came and went. Seasons came and went. Every day was pretty much the same." Ye Qin knew that those few years also didn't go by completely

smoothly for Cheng Feichi and described his own life as lightly as possible. "School's not very different from work anyway. You sing a bit, dance a bit, and get paid. Thinking of it this way, I've been more fortunate than many people."

Just yesterday, Cheng Feichi heard from Liu Yuqing about the various difficulties Ye Qin faced after debuting, including everything that couldn't be searched up—like being slandered by the whole web, signing unfair contracts, and being mistreated by the company. Connecting this to what Zhou Hui had said before, it wasn't hard to figure out how Ye Qin grew a habit of saving up and being frugal.

A while ago, when they went on a trip, they saw a man in black clothes and black sunglasses. Ye Qin blurted out, "Do debt collectors all dress so normally?" Then, he got out his phone, about to call the police. From this, it was evident that this wasn't his first time seeing these kinds of private firms that most people would never come in contact with. Perhaps he'd even had dealings with them before.

In the five years that he was absent, Ye Qin seemed to have changed a lot and, at the same time, not at all. The once-young master that stood out amongst the crowd had taken a roll through the mud until he was covered in dust. And yet, he remained clean and pure on the inside, his passion yet to die out.

Rather than catch Ye Qin in his lies, Cheng Feichi speculated for a while. He looked down at Ye Qin. With his palm touching Ye Qin's slightly pointed chin, he asked, "Really?"

Ye Qin had brainwashed himself long ago and accepted these conditions free of guilt. He laughed, "Really. Those five years went by very quickly, just like taking a nap. I closed my eyes, opened them again, and you came back."

As he talked, he lifted a hand to cover his eyes, and then spread his fingers to look at Cheng Feichi through the cracks to

prove that he was telling the truth.

Ye Qin's eyelashes were long and thick. When they fluttered open suddenly, they were like a small brush sweeping on the heart. Then, he revealed a pair of gleaming eyes that only had Cheng Feichi in them.

As the movie's white text on black background scrolled to an end and the music gradually faded, the two of them, yet to finish, hugged and grinded on the sofa.

That long kiss just now seemed to have spent all of Ye Qin's strength. He lay limply on the sofa with his arms circled around Cheng Feichi's neck, letting Cheng Feichi drop kiss after soft kiss on his lips.

Cheng Feichi held up Ye Qin's body with one hand, caressing every inch of Ye Qin's face with his eyes under the sunlight that came in through the window. He let the strong lines that had been carved permanently in his mind long ago deepen again and again.

For a moment, his eyes were pierced by light without warning. Cheng Feichi squinted slightly and checked hoarsely, "As I came back, you woke up?"

Those submerged in the sea of affection inevitably fell into something known as a whirlpool of greed, cherishing the other above all, but always longing for the other to only see them.

Ye Qin met his gaze and frankly gave him the answer he most wanted to hear, "Yeah. When you kissed me, I woke up."

The corners of Cheng Feichi's mouth ripped into a smile as he asked the man beneath him, "Like Snow White?"

A layer of blush quickly crept over fair skin. Embarrassed again, Ye Qin turned elsewhere. "S-Snow what..."

"Sleeping Beauty then?"

...It was rather more fitting than Snow White.

Ye Qin, who really loved to sleep, got embarrassed to the point where his ears burned. He raised his hands and pushed at

Cheng Feichi's chest. "Alright, alright. It's time for a midday nap."

Cheng Feichi didn't have a habit of taking midday naps, but perhaps the temperature was right or the surroundings were calm. This time he slept.

When Ye Qin woke up, he first stretched a small stretch. Then, he carefully crawled out of the crook of Cheng Feichi's arm. He got on the ground and walked to the window barefoot, opening the curtains just a crack. Then, he poured a glass of warm water and got it ready by the bedside.

After doing this, he crawled back into bed and shrank back into Cheng Feichi's arms as the latter slept on his side. He held up the hand hanging down the side of Cheng Feichi's body, letting the long, narrow beams of light slide across every one of his long fingers until it finally fell on the bony back of his hand. He could almost see through the blue veins to the hot blood quickly rushing through them.

It was a little pretentious to say, but no other words could describe the distinct feeling of realness of the moment. Just holding his hand was like having the whole world.

His world could be very big, so big that the ends couldn't be reached within a lifetime; his world could also be very small, so small that it needed this warm embrace.

Temperatures began to warm up starting from the skin that was stuck together. Ye Qin slowly released a breath and let go of the last bit of importance tied to the past that unintentionally invaded his thoughts.

Very soon, there was something new to fill up the tiny bit of cleared space, as warm as the heat in the palm of one's hand, as bright as the spring lighting outside the window.

Cheng Feichi was his light. He had to take many detours and spent a lot of time to catch him, cherish him, and repay him with the same level of passion.

The hand he was holding onto moved a little and Ye Qin quickly put it back where it was. He found a comfortable position and closed his eyes.

He could sleep for as long as he wanted.

He slashed through thorns and thistles in his dreams, and his prince crossed over lofty mountains and high ranges outside. Eventually his prince would arrive and use a gentle kiss to wake him.

EXTRA 05

Brief Letters of Lasting Love

EARLY in the morning on February 13th, Ye Qin got up and wrote a letter, and then discreetly slipped it under Cheng Feichi's pillow...

My beloved gege,

In the days after the ice and snow melted and new life has grown, allow me to wish you happy birthday, good health, that you're happy every day, and all things go your way with one hundred twenty percent sincerity and passion!

Sure enough, this kind of blessing only feels sincere when written... Tomorrow is Valentine's Day. I'm scared that I won't make it so I turned on the lamp and wrote this at night. (I did it on the down low 'cause I was afraid of waking you so my handwriting will be a bit ugly. Please don't mind)

I forget how many birthdays I spent with you. In any case I'll stay with you from now on, so I won't spend time counting. I don't know why I particularly want to write you a letter this time. Maybe it's because I didn't write enough back when I used to get you breakfast. Also, I never really got to write you a proper... love letter or something like that. This will make up for it.

Speaking of school, I don't know if you remember that girl, Zhang Peiyao? She was from the affiliated high school, a bit taller than me. I heard that she wanted to date you... Ok fine, I didn't "hear." I knew you transferred to No. 6 partly because of her. At the international school exchange, I accidentally overheard you two talk (it really wasn't on purpose).

Recently, I ran into her in a studio. She's in the media business so we might even run into each other in the future. She knows we're together and wants me to tell you "sorry." She said she was young and stupid and made mistakes, and that it's up to you whether you forgive her.

At first, I wanted to tell you this in person, but I never found the chance... Ok, ok. Mostly it's because she tried to get with you so she's my love rival in a way. I'm not nice enough to help vindicate a love rival.

You know that I'm petty. Stay away from those sucker-uppers from now on. No good person would seduce a man with a husband!

Actually, I wrote you this letter because I have some questions I want to ask you, aka two questions I'm too embarrassed to ask in person (can you tell how nervous I am). It's up to you if and how you want to answer. I only have one request, which is to tell the truth. You're not allowed to play it down just to make me happy, or else... Humph!

First, I want to ask if the Three-Cup Chicken I made for New Years tasted bad? After the first bite, you stopped talking. When I asked you if it was good, you just nodded. I was so freaked out. If it tastes bad, just say it straight out. If you don't tell me, how can I improve? I'm determined to become a godly chef of Chinese cuisine!

And after that...are my massages for your hand injury actually effective? The expert who taught me talked it up to the heavens, said if I did it every day then it'll return to normal after two years.

I didn't really believe him, but it should have some effect for relieving the pain, right? Every time I ask you, you say it's good. If it really works, why do you still use your left hand to hold pens and chopsticks?

If it doesn't work, you have to tell me. I'll change my technique. If you feel uncomfortable, you also have to tell me. Sometimes, when I use too much strength, I can't feel it myself. I only see that your hands have turned red after I finish massaging.

You have to tell me!!! You absolutely, absolutely, absolutely can't bear everything alone again. Happiness or pain, I want to share it all with you.

Ah! Now that I finally asked, I feel so relaxed! What's that saying again… the weight on your chest finally lifts?

Oh, right, if you ever want anything, you have to tell me, regardless of if it can be bought with money or not. I like to live a life full of challenges!

If you're really too embarrassed to say, then I'll first demonstrate asking you for something, haha. I want to go back to the aquarium, find a place away from the crowd (those little kids are *too* noisy). When I was little, mom and dad were always busy. They never took me out to have fun and made me unable to write those "my happy day spent with mom and dad" essays.

If only I knew you when I was a kid. Then I could write "my happy day spent with my gege." So what do you say to going back? We'll plan out a time and spend an entire day there stuffing the seals with food!

Oh, right, my teacher knows about our relationship, so you don't have to keep calling yourself a parent… He even asked why we didn't invite him to the wedding fest. I said we already got married back in high school and he was dumbstruck. Hahahahah!

I didn't realize I wrote so much, and it's all just ramblings. Actually, apart from science, my worst subject is Chinese, so bad

I went off topic on my college entrance exam essays...

It's really late. Let's leave it here for today.

I hope that I can write you a letter every year from now on as your wife (strike-through) husband. I'm sealing the letter. I hope I'll see your birthday wishes (the heartfelt ones) in your reply.

Gege, happy birthday. I love you. I love you forever and ever and ever. ♥

Yours lovely, YQ

Late into the night on February 13th, Cheng Feichi slipped the reply under Ye Qin's pillow before giving the little guy, soundly asleep, a soft kiss on the forehead.

My dear Ye Xiaoruan,

I got your letter. Thank you for preparing this surprise for me. I had a very happy birthday this year.

As a matter of fact, I also have not written a letter in a long time. The last time was in reply to a certain little guy who got me breakfast many years ago. Since you called it a love letter, then let's just consider it that.

If we count those five years, then this is our eighth year together. I don't have a habit of celebrating my birthday, but as long as you like it, I'll remember to come home early every year from now on.

If you hadn't mentioned it, I would have forgotten Zhang Peiyao. She was my classmate in the affiliated high school. I tutored her for a while. After I got the feeling that she was having thoughts other than studying, I began to avoid her, so you don't have to dwell on this part of the past. If you happen to see her again, tell her not to think about this anymore for me.

Also, help me tell a certain little guy to let the past be the past. If he always worries about it, he will hurt, and I will hurt.

Just like his blessings for me, I also wish that he is happy every day and all things go his way.

Additionally, this is a normal reaction, not pettiness. If he didn't get jealous that day, I'd get worried.

Now I'll answer the questions.

First, the Three-Cup-Chicken you made was really good, balanced between salty and sweet and improved a lot from the sweet and sour ribs you made for Christmas before that. I didn't say anything because I choked on chilis and didn't want to scare you by speaking. You're very sensitive when it comes to your cooking. If I coughed, you surely would have thought that the food wasn't good, blame yourself, and get upset. I don't want you to deny your abilities.

Cooking is a happy thing, especially when you make food for someone else. Seeing others eat happily gives you a heartfelt feeling of being blessed. And so, there's no need to force yourself to do stuff you're not good at. You're already very talented. You know how to sing and dance and you're sunshiny and cute. There are so many fans who love you.

The light you give off from the inside is the brightest star in the night sky.

The injury on my right hand is not as serious as you think. After going through rehabilitation, it pretty much healed and doesn't affect daily life. I use my left hand often because I got used to it in the process of healing. Actually, I have no problem writing and using chopsticks with my right hand. You should be able to feel whether this hand is useful or not when I put it on your body.

Of course your massages are effective. At least, I feel very good. You don't need to worry about using too much force. To me, your massage is the same as tickling. The redness is not due to pain.

I love listening every time you tell stories while pressing down. What will you say tonight? I'm already looking forward to it.

I promise that I answered honestly above, though I'm still very curious about the contents that come after "or else." If I lied, how would you have punished me?

Writing letters really does help communicate things that are normally hard to bring up out of embarrassment. Right now, I also kind of feel like a weight has been lifted from my chest. I hope you understand that I'm not only capable of sharing happiness with you and not pain. There are some things that I don't bring up because there is no reason to dwell on them. I'm more concerned about the present and want to make sure every day I spend with you is a good one.

As for the things I want, what you give me is already enough. To me, family and love are the two most extravagant things in the world, and you've given me both.

Though if we're speaking of specific requests like "going back to the aquarium," I do have one. Last semester, you didn't pass your university English course. Your teacher said if you fail again, it will affect your graduation. How about doing a test before bed after you give your hand massage today? Don't worry, I won't deliberately come up with questions outside the syllabus to make things hard for you.

Speaking of the aquarium, last time was my first time going. Thankfully I had you to introduce those marine animals. If you want to go again, I'll make time as much as possible and study ahead, so you won't feel bored this time.

Actually, based on this letter, I can't tell that you go off topic in your essays. There must have been other factors at the time that impacted your articulation. My Chinese is not very good either. If I wrote the national college exams with you that year, I probably also would have gone off topic.

Of course, if you think you're lacking in any aspect, you can never go wrong with practicing more. For example, when we

come back from the aquarium, you can write an essay with "my happy day spent with my gege" as the topic. I am very willing to be the only person other than you to who sees this essay.

Right now, it is 11:50 on February 13th. You're curled up on the bed, sleeping like a piglet. Did you stay up really late yesterday to prepare the surprise?

Thank you, my darling.

I only have one birthday wish. I wish that in the next year, the year after, the year after that...and in every year, you'll be by my side at this moment.

Yours lovely, CF

EXTRA 06

100 Q&A

CHENG Feichi and Ye Qin's event:

1. Name?
YQ: Ye Qin.
CF: Cheng Feichi.

2. Age?
YQ: You go first.
CF: 26.
YQ: A little younger than him.

3. Gender?
YQ: Male.
CF: Mmhm.

4. How would you describe your personality?
YQ: How would I describe...
CF: Normal.
YQ: Yeah, pretty normal.

5. And his personality?

YQ: Perfect. Per-fect. Is that how you say it?

CF: Mmhm, very good.

6. When did you meet? Where?

YQ: The corner shop in front of High School No. 6. He was moving stuff.

CF: The convenience store on Yulin Street. He was—

YQ: *[interrupting]* I-I was looking for trouble.

7. What was your first impression of him?

YQ: Do you want the truth, or...

CF: The truth.

YQ: Tall, handsome, not like a straight-A student.

CF: Then what was I like?

YQ: My future husband.

[CF laughs.]

YQ: Your first impression of me...wasn't good, was it?

CF: It wasn't bad. A young master who still hadn't grown up.

8. What's one thing you like about him?

YQ: Everything!

CF: He's soft-hearted and innocent.

YQ: That's two things.

CF: Mmhm. And cute.

9. What's one thing you hate about him?

YQ: Nothing. I like everything!

CF: Nothing.

YQ: Actually, there's something, but not strong enough to call hate.

[CF is confused.]

YQ: Uh...he hides his worries too much. He won't tell me even if I ask.

CF: Some things, you don't need to know.

YQ: You see? You see? ╲(ˇ ▽ ˇ)╱

10. Do you think you're a good match for each other?

YQ: Very good.

CF: Yes.

11. What do you call him?

YQ: Gege~

CF: Ye Qin.

YQ: Hmm?

CF: Ye Xiaoruan.

YQ: Hey!

12. What do you want him to call you?

YQ: Anything. I'm not picky.

CF: Anything.

13. What animal would he be?

YQ: A tortoise.

CF: Why a tortoise?

YQ: They're long-lived.

[CF is speechless.]

YQ: A lion, then!

[CF is confused.]

YQ: They're mighty!

[CF laughs.]

YQ: What do you think I am?

CF: A cat.

YQ: I knew it.

14. If you were to give each other gifts, what would you give?

YQ: A house, a car, a watch...everything.

CF: It depends on what he needs.

15. Then what would you want as a present?

YQ: Anything.

CF: Nothing in particular.

16. Are you unhappy with anything about him? Like what?

YQ: Didn't we just answer this? Next question.

[CF nods.]

17. What's wrong with you?

YQ: *[puzzled]* What's wrong with this question?!

CF: You should ask him.

18. What's wrong with the other person?

YQ: Nothing.

CF: *[laughing]* Nothing.

19. What kind of things does he do to make you unhappy?

YQ: Uh... When he's clearly upset but won't say anything.

CF: Same as him.

YQ: Huh? I'm the most open person in the world!

[CF shakes his head in disagreement.]

20. What is it you do that makes him unhappy?

YQ: Is this question any different from the last?

CF: No.

YQ: Next question then.

21. How close have you gotten?

YQ: Do you even need to ask?

CF: Next question.

22. Where was your first date?

YQ: A movie at Times Square Plaza.

CF: Mmhm.

YQ: I was smiling like an idiot. He was completely expressionless.

CF: As long as you were happy.

23. How were the vibes between you then?

YQ: Well, uh...pretty warm?

CF: Mmhm.

24. How far did you go?

YQ: We just started dating. How far could we go?

CF: I took him home.

YQ: Wait, didn't I take you home?

CF: Think more carefully.

YQ: Oh... Oh!

25. Where do you often go for dates?

YQ: All kinds of restaurants, and I keep him company while he works.

CF: That doesn't count as a date.

YQ: Oh, right. I was pursuing you back then. Let's see, date spot... Then, High School No. 6!

CF: Mmm.

26. What would you do for his birthday?

YQ: Prepare gifts? Balloons, cake...everything fun!

CF: Take a day off and spend it with him.

27. Who confessed first?

YQ: Me! Me! Me!

CF: Him.

28. How much do you like him?

YQ: What kind of stupid question is this?

CF: More than he can tell.

YQ: Then, me too!

29. Then do you love him?

YQ: More the stupid questions.

CF: Yes.

30. What does he say to leave you speechless?

YQ: Anything. Everything. All of it.

CF: Heartfelt words.

31. If you suspect his feelings have changed, what would you do?

YQ: Observe my rival and become more competitive.

CF: Never thought about it before.

32. Can you forgive him for changing his feelings?

YQ: *[after a pause]* Yes.

CF: I've never thought about it before.

YQ: So superficial...

CF: I really haven't. There's no need for these hypotheticals either.

YQ: Okay then. (o__)/

33. If he was more than an hour late on a date, what would you do?

YQ: Call the police. He's never late.

CF: Call him.

YQ: What if I don't pick up?

CF: I'll look for your assistant.

YQ: What if she also doesn't pick up?

CF: I'll go out and look.

YQ: What if you can't find me?

CF: That won't happen.

YQ: I wish I also had that kind of confidence. (·_·)

34. What do you like the most about his body?

YQ: With a gege like him, I like it all!

CF: His eyes.

YQ: Meaning you don't like my nose, lips, waist, and legs?

CF: *[laughing]* No, I like it all.

35. What kind of expression does he make that's sexy?

YQ: Everything. Everything is "sex."

CF: It's "sexy."

YQ: Then what does "sex" mean?

CF: I'll tell you when we get home.

YQ: Then, what's my sexiest expression?

CF: I'll tell you when we get home.

36. When you two are together, what makes your heart beat the fastest?

YQ: C-c-can this kind of thing be said in broad daylight?

CF: No.

YQ: Then we'll talk about it at home.

37. Have you ever lied to him? Do you lie often?

YQ: *[after a pause]* Would anyone believe me if I say I didn't lie often?

CF: I would.

38. When do you feel the most blessed?

YQ: As long as I'm with him, I feel blessed doing anything.

CF: Mmhm.

39. Have you ever fought before?

YQ: Uh...

CF: Once in a while.

YQ: Yesterday and the day before yesterday, weren't we still...

CF: Hm?

YQ: Okay, since you don't count that as fighting, never mind. Next question!

40. What do you fight about?

YQ: It's usually just me fighting.

[YQ makes incoherent noises.]

CF: He doesn't anymore.

41. How do you make up after?

YQ: I shamelessly pester him to forgive me.

CF: I just wait for him to calm down.

42. Do you still hope to be lovers in the next life?

YQ: Of course!

CF: Yes.

43. When do you feel loved by him?

YQ: When he smiles at me.

CF: Lots of times.

44. How do you show your love?
YQ: I say it out loud!
CF: I treat him well.

45. When do you feel like "he doesn't love me anymore"?
YQ: When he...said that he was breaking up with me.
CF: I once thought this at a certain time, but afterward I knew it wasn't true.
YQ: I was wrong... 〒▽〒
CF: It's all in the past.

46. What flower suits him in your opinion?
YQ: A peony.
[CF is confused.]
YQ: The king of all flowers. What flower am I? Tell me! Tell me!
CF: A sunflower.
YQ: Ha ha ha. I'm so happy. I thought I'd be a poisonous flower, like oleander or something.
[CF is speechless.]

47. Have you ever hidden anything from him?
YQ: Right now, I don't...think so.
CF: Yes.
[YQ is shocked.]
YQ: What?!
CF: It's not important.
YQ: I'm so mad right now.

48. What makes you feel inferior?

YQ: I'm not as tall as him or as handsome as him, and I don't earn as much as him.

CF: I'm not as likable as him.

YQ: Really? I don't believe you.

CF: Really.

49. Is your relationship public or secret?

YQ: Public!

CF: Mmhm.

50. Do you think your love for him will last forever?

YQ: I worked my ass off to get this guy. Why wouldn't it?

CF: Yes.

51. Are you the gong or the shou?

YQ: Uh...

[CF gives him a look, as if telling him to go first.]

YQ: Shou...

CF: Hm?

YQ: Shou!

[CF nods.]

52. How did you decide this?

YQ: *[coming to a realization]* Right, how did we decide this?

CF: Natural course.

YQ: Right, natural course...

53. Are you satisfied with the current arrangement?

YQ: It's...not bad.

[CF gives him a look, as if telling him to think again.]

YQ: Yes! I'm very satisfied!

CF: I'm satisfied.

54. Where did you first have sex?

YQ: Are we allowed to talk about this?

CF: The Jiayuan Compound.

YQ: A specific apartment in the Jiayuan Compound.

55. How did you feel?

YQ: Are we allowed to talk about this?

[CF gives him a look, as if telling him that he wants to know.]

YQ: *[blushing]* Okay... It was quite good.

CF: Same for me.

56. What did he look like?

YQ: I'm not telling you.

CF: Cute.

YQ: I remember I was very noisy.

CF: You were good.

57: The morning after your first time, what were your first words?

YQ: *[looking to the sky]* Who'd remember that?

CF: Does it still hurt?

YQ: *[blushing harder]* See? You know what this is called? Textbook "afterthought"!

58. How many times do you have sex in a week?

YQ: *[counting with his fingers]* One, two, three, four, five...

CF: We can't talk about this.

YQ: *[covering his own mouth]* Yea, yea, we gant dalk aboud diss.

59. Ideally, how many times do you want to have sex in a week?

YQ: Anything goes.

CF: Anything goes. Whatever he wants.

60. Then how do you have sex?

YQ: Which time?

CF: Next question.

61. What's your most sensitive area?

[YQ looks at CF.]

CF: There are many.

YQ: *[startling]* But you don't have any sensitive places!

CF: I do.

YQ: Where?

CF: Anywhere you've touched before.

YQ: *[blushing for the third time]* Oh. Oh.

62. What's his most sensitive area?

YQ: Is this any different from the previous question?

CF: No.

YQ: Next question!

63. Use one sentence to describe your partner during sex.

YQ: One sentence is not enough.

[CF gives him a look that indicates he should please elaborate.]

YQ: *[looking away]* He's just, *sexy*, okay!

CF: *[smiling]* He's very cute.

YQ: Can't you use an adjective other than "cute"?

CF: Mmm.

64. Speaking frankly, do you like sex?

YQ: *[embarrassed]* If it's him...then yes.

CF: Same.

65. Where do you normally have sex?

YQ: In bed.

[CF gives him a look that indicates he should think about it more carefully.]

YQ: *[blushing for the fourth time]* U-uh, we really do mostly do it on the bed!

[CF nods.]

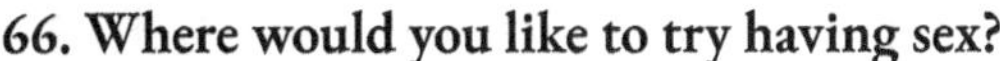

66. Where would you like to try having sex?

YQ: Let me think...

CF: Wherever he wants.

YQ: *[skeptical]* You've never thought about this?

CF: I have.

YQ: Where? Where?

CF: I'll tell you when we get home.

67. Do you shower before sex or after?

YQ: Both, obviously. How uncomfortable is it being all sweaty?

[CF nods.]

68. Do you have any agreements for when you have sex?

YQ: No. I think...

CF: Last time you told me that when you yell "no," it means "keep going"...

YQ: *[covering his mouth]* You really can't talk about that!

69. Have you ever had sexual relations with someone other than your boyfriend?

YQ: No. I'm an ultra-pure boy.

CF: No.

70. Do you agree or disagree with the sentiment that "even

if I can't have their heart, at least I can have their body"?

YQ: It's actually pretty exciting if you think about it?

CF: I disagree.

71. If he was raped by a thug, what would you do?

YQ: I'm sorry, what?! Chop off the thug's dick.

CF: With me here, that kind of thing won't happen.

72. Do you feel embarrassed before sex? Or after?

YQ: A little...

CF: No.

YQ: Bullshit. Last time you were blushing.

CF: Which time?

YQ: You know, when I was crossdre—*ahem*. That time.

CF: That was because it was too hot inside.

YQ: *[curling his lip]* I don't believe you.

73. If a good friend told you, "I'm very lonely, so please, just for tonight..." and wanted you to have sex with them, would you?

YQ: Good friend? Like Zhou Feng?

[CF gives him a look that indicates he should please elaborate.]

YQ: I'm kidding. Zhou Feng only sends me those kinds of messages on April Fool's.

CF: I don't have friends who I can joke around with like that.

74. Do you think you're good at sex?

YQ: I've never compared. How would I know?

CF: You'd have to ask him.

YQ: *[embarrassed for the second time]* You're a...natural?

75. Then what about him?

YQ: I already answered that.
CF: Quite good.
YQ: Really?
CF: You should know based on my reaction.
YQ: *[looking at the sky]* Oh. Oh.

76. What do you want your partner to say during sex?

YQ: Baby, you're so pretty~
CF: Really?
YQ: I was joking.
CF: I want you to tell me how you really feel.
YQ: *[embarrassed for the third time]* Who can actually say that out loud…?

77. What kind of expression do you enjoy seeing on your partner during sex?

YQ: As long as he's looking at me, anything.
CF: Anything.

78. Do you think it's okay to have sex with people other than your boyfriend?

YQ: No. No. No.
CF: No.

79. Do you have any interest in BDSM?

YQ: It's actually pretty exciting if you think about it?
CF: *[after being enlightened on what BDSM is]* It depends on him.
YQ: *[very excitedly]* Then, tonight I want to *[beep]*, and then *[beep]*, and finally *[beep]*!
CF: Okay.

80. If your partner suddenly stops seeking your body, what would you do?

YQ: Lose weight.

CF: Work out.

YQ: Wow! A rare agreement!

81. What are your thoughts on rape?

YQ: Arrest the rapist. Chop off his dick.

CF: It's a criminal offense.

82. Is there anything painful during sex?

YQ: Probably the prep work.

CF: No.

YQ: Then you help me prep from now on.

CF: When have I not?

YQ: The first time!

83. In all the times so far, where have you had sex that made you feel the most excited and anxious?

YQ: That time in his office...

CF: Mmhm.

84. Has the shou ever tempted you first?

CF: Yes.

YQ: It seems to always be me who tempts you first...

85. What was the gong's expression?

YQ: Like, the same as usual.

CF: It wasn't the same.

YQ: You couldn't have seen your own face.

CF: I didn't feel the same.

YQ: *[curious]* What did you feel?

CF: I'll tell you when we go back.

86. Has the gong ever committed rape?
YQ: Of course not.
CF: No.

87. What was the shou's reaction?
YQ: Pass on this question.

88. What is your ideal sex partner like?
YQ: *[pointing next to him]* Like this.
CF: Same as him.

89. Does your current partner match your ideal?
YQ: Perfectly!
CF: Yes.

90. Have you ever used toys during sex?
YQ: Now that you mention this, I seem to be getting new ideas...
CF: No.

91. When was your first time?
YQ: Didn't we answer this already? Pass.

92. Is your partner from then your current boyfriend?
YQ: Of course.
CF: Yes.

93. Where do you like being kissed the most?
YQ: [leaning over and whispering] Behind the ear, collarbone, thigh...I like it all.

[CF nods.]
YQ: What about you?
CF: Anywhere.
YQ: Then next time I'll suck on your fingers and poke you in where it tickles?
[CF says nothing.]

94. Where do you like kissing him the most?

YQ: His palm.
CF: A lot of places.

95. What pleases him the most during sex?

YQ: Probably...when I cry out?
[CF nods.]
YQ: You don't need to answer, gege. Everything you do pleases me.

96. What do you think about during sex?

YQ: How would I still be able to think?
CF: Nothing.

97. How many times do you have sex in one night?

YQ: *[again, somehow]* One, two, three, four...
CF: Depends.

98. When you have sex, do you take off your clothes or does your partner?

YQ: Both have happened. I like to help him strip.
CF: Mmhm.
YQ: Does "mmhm" mean that you like it or that you don't like it?
CF: I like it.

99. To you, sex is?

YQ: A two-person exercise that brings you closer together.

CF: The icing on the cake.

100. Please say one sentence to your boyfriend.

YQ: Gege, I love you!

CF: *[smiling]* I love you, too.

EXTRA 07

After Another Year

- **Pick Up from Work**

On days Ye Qin got off work early or didn't have work, he was very happy to undertake the role of the man of the household and pick up the other man of the household.

Normally, he waited in the lobby of the company, bundled up completely in a mask and hat. He was a public figure, after all, and it wouldn't be good to cause a scene.

However, this was pretty excessive. After he moved his work to S-City, President Cheng had been busy every day and the company employees worked around the clock with him. People were in a rush all around and didn't forget to flip through files with a grave expression even while taking a sip of water. Every time Ye Qin saw them, he lamented the hardship of company slaves.

Cheng Feichi didn't get off work on time again. Ye Qin, waiting more than an hour for him, sampled all the snacks in the tea room. He was still burping by the time he got in the car.

"Are you still eating dinner?" Cheng Feichi asked.

"Yes." Ye Qin rubbed his tummy. "You can't make a meal out of snacks."

Cheng Feichi smiled.

On the road, Ye Qin sought benefits for the employees and recommended a few tasty, inexpensive snacks to Cheng Feichi.

"I'll send this to the Logistics Department and have them prepare," Cheng Feichi said after patiently listening.

When Ye Qin came to pick him up from work again, he found that the snacks in the tea room had indeed been changed to the ones he had recommended.

The Logistics Department also found that the snacks in the tea room disappeared a lot faster than before.

Picking up from work changed from Ye Qin waiting for Cheng Feichi, busy with work, to Cheng Feichi waiting for Ye Qin, busy eating.

One day, on the way back with a full stomach, Ye Qin pinched his tummy with a sour face. "I've fattened myself up."

"Mmhm. You've fattened up my workers too," Cheng Feichi approved.

- **Keeping Plants**

Ye Qin accepted a new role as a sullen, introverted shut-in in a suspense drama.

Because this role was the complete opposite of who he was as a person, Ye Qin began preparing very early on. He let his hair grow out, changed the way he spoke and the clothes he wore, and even developed some shut-in habits.

Playing video games was too noisy, not sullen enough. Piecing Lego together cost too much money and didn't match the stingy personality. After closely examining the script, Ye Qin decided to keep a few plants.

He first bought two that were said to be very hardy and easy to keep. When he searched for care instructions online, some

other plants were promoted to him and he bought a few more.

Then he had coincidentally been added into a plant lover group chat and bought a plant rack. Together with friends in the group, he bought a plant rack, various spray bottles, various fertilizers, nutrient solutions, insecticides...just like developing an actual interest.

The apartment that Cheng Feichi and Ye Qin lived in had one living room and two rooms, one was a bedroom and the other a study. Occasionally, Cheng Feichi did work in the study.

The two of them originally had more than enough space, but ever since Ye Qin fell into the plant hole, there were plants spread from the balcony to the dining table. One day, Cheng Feichi carried his laptop into the study and kicked a pot three times in the distance of six steps. He managed to get to the desk just to find that there was also a plant on the chair.

"*Monstera deliciosa* need light. It won't get good light if it's on the floor," Ye Qin explained and then promised, "I'll just put it on the chair during the day. I'll take it away before you come back, I promise!"

But Cheng Feichi told him, "Don't worry. Just leave it there."

So Ye Qin did without qualms, and it was left there until the drama began filming.

The day before going on set, Ye Qin handwrote a plant care guidebook with precise details down to the humidity, temperature, and the circumstances in which the plants needed watering. Afraid Cheng Feichi couldn't tell them apart, he even hung a little tag on the stem of every plant so that they could be matched.

Cheng Feichi took on this heavy responsibility.

While he was on set, Ye Qin had to video call Cheng Feichi almost every day; before, it was to see him, and now, to see the plants.

"Go left. Let me see my green velvet alocasia. Wait, no. Go

back a bit. Get closer. Let me see how the leaves are... And that begonia in the corner. It's the most finicky..."

Cheng Feichi was patient. Whenever he was home, he would hold up the phone and let Ye Qin see as much as he wanted.

There was only one time, after Ye Qin finished looking, that he didn't end the call. Lips pursed and silent, he just looked at Ye Qin in stillness.

This put Ye Qin in a bit of a panic as he looked at the person in the front camera. "What is it? Did I grow something on my face?"

Cheng Feichi shook his head.

"Then what?"

Seeing as Ye Qin's head was filled with plants, Cheng Feichi gave a light sigh. "It's time for bed," he reminded.

Only then did Ye Qin remember to lean over, kissing the camera fiercely. "I almost forgot. Goodnight, gege!"

When it hit him that his gege had been jealous of his plants, Ye Qin's unhideable tail shot up to the sky.

On the car ride back from set, he grinned from ear to ear as he watched Cheng Feichi drive. When Cheng Feichi asked why he was smiling, he raised his eyebrows and said, "Nothing. I'm just seeing how my gege misses me while I'm gone."

Cheng Feichi didn't reply to that. When they got back to the capital, he didn't take them home, but to another newly developed building.

The trees cast shade all over the ground. Cars and people were going about. This was one of the best compounds.

They went into an Italian-style apartment on the top floor of a building. The place was neither big nor small: three bedrooms, two living rooms, and a ten-meter balcony. The first thing that could be seen was a giant window wall that allowed for excellent lighting.

Ye Qin was stunned. Then, he got a bit annoyed. "Didn't we

agree that I'd buy the next place?"

"Yes, you can buy the next one," Cheng Feichi dismissed with little effort.

Despite the ire in his words, as Ye Qin looked around, he couldn't help but start planning—the biggest room would be the bedroom, the one beside it the study, and the smallest would be perfect for keeping plants.

Well, upon closer examination, not exactly perfect...

Ye Qin roughly measured the size of the room with his steps before taking out his phone and scrolling through the plants he had just bought online. He then thought of the Legos at home, piled into mountains, and put a hand on his forehead.

And so Cheng Feichi beckoned him to ascend the wooden stairs onto the top floor and open the only door there.

As blinding rays of sun shot inside, green filled his eyes as far as they could see.

All of Ye Qin's plants had been transferred here, taking up less than half of the space on the balcony. The other half contained a glass greenhouse that had already been set up, and a few tropical plants had their leaves stretched out inside, looking quite comfortable.

Ye Qin was so dumbfounded he couldn't even make a complete sentence. "T-t-this..."

"The balcony is counted in the square footage. It's not illegal," Cheng Feichi dispelled his underlying worry.

"I-I know." Ye Qin straightened out his tongue. "You didn't buy this for my plants, did you?"

"Do you like it?" Cheng Feichi asked, not answering.

"Of course!" Ye Qin nodded like a knife dicing garlic.

Ye Qin watered a few plants as he admired the balcony. When they went back inside, he grabbed onto Cheng Feichi.

They say water in the distance cannot dispel thirst. After

four months without touch, Ye Qin's body heated fervently just holding hands.

Perhaps deliberately, perhaps not, Cheng Feichi's expression expressed doubt at being grabbed. "What's wrong?"

"T-the plants were just watered." Ye Qin's eyes drifted everywhere else as he avoided the subject. "Now it's...turn."

"Whose turn?" Cheng Feichi asked with a doubtful expression.

Unable to hold back any longer, Ye Qin shut his eyes and gathered his resolve. "My turn. You should water me now!"

Right after he said this, he felt his world turn upside down. When Ye Qin opened his eyes, he was already being pushed into the new bed in the new bedroom of their new home.

He suddenly realized that he'd been positively duped, but he felt smug at knowing that his charm was working. "Hmph, I knew you..."

This time, he couldn't even finish before the face in front of him magnified and Cheng Feichi's kiss pressed down impatiently, like a yearning that'd long begun to overflow.

• Renovations

Even though the new place was well-decorated, the developer and the owner inevitably had different tastes. And so, after moving, Ye Qin rolled up his sleeves and began renovations.

Refashioning, to be precise. Many of the fixtures couldn't be removed. They took apart the suspended ceiling and changed the plaster. They also smashed up the bathroom and redid it to suit their cleansing routines. They installed two sinks in one and a bathtub in another, the kind that could easily fit two people.

Ye Qin didn't need to do anything himself, but doing renovations meant that inevitably, dust flew everywhere.

In this period, Cheng Feichi came home every day to see Ye

Qin's face covered in dirt.

They laid out bricks on the balcony, and Ye Qin even put on a safety hat, tapping each brick one by one to check for empty spaces like a construction foreman.

He was still tapping by the time Cheng Feichi came back. When he couldn't hear the difference, he laid his ear on the bricks and tapped two repeatedly to compare the sound.

"I heard our neighbor group Ning Lan say his captain has perfect pitch. If only I had it too," Ye Qin said as he tapped, regretting that he hadn't learned piano properly.

Cheng Feichi crouched down, wiping the dust on his face for him. "You don't need to be so careful. If they break down the road, we'll re-lay them."

"No, no, no." Ye Qin shook his head in fear. "Let's just be careful now. Renos are so annoying. Once is enough."

The home study, which was pretty much only used by Cheng Feichi, was also renovated according to Ye Qin's plans.

Ye Qin personally took a trip to Building Materials City to choose latex paint, changed the soundproof windows, picked out the curtains after closely examining the way they shaded and draped. When he got home, he put them in the washing machine first before installing them.

When Cheng Feichi came back on that day, Ye Qin took him to the study and asked him what was different.

Cheng Feichi saw right away. "The chair."

"Correct!" Ye Qin pushed Cheng Feichi by the shoulders and urged him to try it out. "I spent a lot of time picking it out. This ergonomic chair is exceptional in terms of looks, comfort, and weight-bearing capacity."

Desperately wanting to be praised, Ye Qin had been looking closely at Cheng Feichi's expression, so when Cheng Feichi's lower lip tugged up the tiniest bit at "weight-bearing

capacity," he caught it.

"What are you smiling at?" Ye Qin didn't understand. "What's wrong with a good weight-bearing capacity?"

Cheng Feichi lifted his eyelids, looking at Ye Qin, and sure enough, there was an ambiguous smile in his eyes too.

This look, this scene—Ye Qin immediately thought of that winter when he indulged in Cheng Feichi's office. That chair, it seemed to have been the exact same.

A deep blush flew across his cheeks, and he turned to flee, but Cheng Feichi grabbed him by the arm and pulled him back. His body leaned back and his ass landed on Cheng Feichi's lap.

...Now he was even more like a little office worker seducing the boss.

Compared to Ye Qin, who was so embarrassed he wanted nothing more than to dig a hole and crawl inside, Cheng Feichi asked calmly and openly, "Do you remember?"

"Remember what?" Ye Qin pretended to be dumb.

To remind him, the two of them reenacted what happened back then in detail for the next two hours.

Afterwards, Ye Qin was both tired and blissed out, and he didn't forget to open that orange app and give the ergonomic chair a five-star review.

As they talked in bed, Cheng Feichi told Ye Qin not to tire himself out with renovations and to take his time.

"No way." Ye Qin shook his head. "We already agreed..."

His sentence drifted off. Cheng Feichi turned over. "Agreed?"

"You never repeat something good," Ye Qin declared smugly, regaining ground.

Unfortunately, Cheng Feichi had an outstanding memory, and it didn't take long for him to get a semblance of recollection. "Ohhhh, the dowry."

He obviously stretched out the "oh" on purpose.

Ye Qin turned his back on him and covered his face in deep embarrassment.

Cheng Feichi dug him out in no time and gave him a long kiss.

When Ye Qin questioned him afterwards, Cheng Feichi admitted that he really liked the renovations.

When Ye Qin asked him what he liked, he said, "Everything."

Ye Qin muttered under his breath, resenting his half-heartedness.

"For real, I like it all," Cheng Feichi said more seriously than usual, looking into Ye Qin's eyes. "Our home is becoming better and better."

More and more like a home.

• A Wedding

After moving in and inviting Liao Yifang over for hotpot, Zhou Feng tagged along as a plus one.

They got a project as a housewarming gift, which Ye Qin found a place to put in the living room. While Cheng Feichi busied himself in the kitchen, he climbed the ladder armed with an electric drill and installed it in a jiffy.

Bearing witness from start to finish, Zhou Hui couldn't help but clap and cheer. "Qin-ge, if you ever lose your job, you can become a renovator. I'll do it with you."

"Asshole." Ye Qin rolled his eyes in return.

They started up the projector and began sharing old photos to "commemorate the past and celebrate the present."

Among them were those that Zhou Feng had taken of campus life in high school. Liao Yifang appeared most frequently on camera, followed by Ye Qin and their buddies. Once in a while, half of Cheng Feichi's face could be found in a corner.

"What is this? He's barely in any photos," Ye Qin expressed his dissatisfaction.

Now it was Zhou Feng's time to roll his eyes. "If I took pictures of the straight-A student all the time, you would have killed me."

Just as they got to Liao Yifang and Zhou Feng's wedding photos, Cheng Feichi came out of the kitchen.

Ye Qin was quite taken in and infected by the smiles they had in the photos. Recalling the lively scene, he stared at the screen and sighed very quietly.

One month later, after Ye Qin finished a magazine cover shoot, Cheng Feichi told him they were going somewhere when he came to pick him up in his car.

Ye Qin jolted. "Did you buy another house?"

Cheng Feichi just smiled.

They arrived at an empty field without a single light, and Ye Qin grabbed onto Cheng Feichi's arm tightly, scared he would get lost.

He wasn't stupid. He knew there would be a surprise based on the situation. Cheng Feichi, who wore a three piece suit every day, clearly dressed meticulously today. He even wore the necktie that Ye Qin picked out for him last time.

Ye Qin quickly looked down at his shoes. Thankfully, he'd dressed formally for the photoshoot today, a casual white suit that somehow matched Cheng Feichi's black one.

Ye Qin couldn't resist making all sorts of guesses as they walked inside, but he was wrong in all of them. Cheng Feichi had given him a house, a car, and didn't really need to come here to give him other gifts.

The wind suddenly whistled past his ears, rustling the leaves. At this blessing, Ye Qin suddenly had a thought and tapped his head. "You didn't buy me a plant, did you? We've got

too many at home. We're running out of space."

Cheng Feichi was speechless.

When the lights lit up in front of him like the sky of stars coming out from the clouds, and his good friends appeared in a dream-like scene, Ye Qin was rendered speechless. It was ages before he realized that Cheng Feichi prepared a wedding for him.

A garden party wedding, to be precise.

It wasn't as strict as a traditional wedding. A park with clean air was chosen as the location, and strings of lights were wrapped around trees and railings everywhere. The multicolor balloons and fresh flowers were even more dazzling.

Beautiful music lingered in his ears and a sweet scent pervaded the air. All the honored guests in attendance were dressed casually, running around everywhere. Some took photos under the arch covered with flowers, others smiled and made small talk next to the table with fruits and cake.

Liao Yifang and Zhou Feng were in the middle of blowing up balloons. When they saw Ye Qin, they greeted him normally. "I'm so tired of blowing these. Come help!"

And so Ye Qin became the first groom in history to blow up balloons for himself to decorate his own wedding.

The other groom also joined in, blowing a long one. He twisted it into a perfect heart and handed it to Ye Qin.

"Today is our wedding anniversary." It was rare for Cheng Feichi's voice to waver. "We didn't have a wedding ceremony back then, so this is to make up for it. I hope..."

Impatient, Ye Qin snatched the heart and answered at lightning speed, "I like it. I really, really like it."

It's impossible for me not to like anything from you.

As part of the warm and lively occasion, they made the vows as holy and dignified as any wedding.

The priest hired by Cheng Feichi had also officiated Liao

Yifang and Zhou Feng's wedding. It was said that newlyweds blessed by him were joined at the lips in loving harmony and didn't even bicker, let alone raise the topic of divorce.

Ye Qin was impatient even with a mere formality. Before the priest even finished, he said, "I do," drawing laughs from everyone off-stage.

On Cheng Feichi's side, things couldn't speed up enough. Time seemed to slow down. When he finished hearing the priest read out the vows, he was still standing in place with no sign of speaking.

He stood for so long that Ye Qin's heart began to pound. *Is he having regrets?* he thought in trepidation. *Why hasn't he spoken? Is he waiting for someone to snatch him?*

To someone as stingy as Ye Qin when it came to feelings, all their friends attending the wedding could be potential enemies who would snatch away Cheng Feichi.

Just when Ye Qin couldn't wait any longer and was about to answer for him, Cheng Feichi looked at him and suddenly said, "Apart from owing you a wedding, I seem to also owe you something else."

Ye Qin blinked. Before he could figure out what those words meant, Cheng Feichi grabbed his hand with the ring on and slowly got to one knee in front of him.

"I also owe you a proposal." Despite his smiling expression, Cheng Feichi's tones was even more earnest and solemn than the priest's. "Ye Qin, will you marry me?

"Will you stay by my side from now on, trust me, depend on me, be with me through the good times and the bad, share with me both happiness and sorrow?"

For some reason, when they came from Cheng Feichi's mouth, these words that were similar in meaning had the power to move earth.

They made his heart tremble, took his soul from his body.

Ye Qin clearly never expected this moment. He even thought, most of the time, that this kind of wedding ceremony announcing their marriage to the whole world was unnecessary for the two of them. But somehow, right now, he was still touched.

Perhaps it made more sense to say that he was moved.

So many times now that he lost count.

Ye Qin swallowed a mouthful of empty air to clear up his slightly blurry vision.

He saw bright lights and himself, surrounded by flowers, in Cheng Feichi's amber eyes.

The man in front of him was no different from when they were young. Handsome, smart, and steady was what everyone could see on the outside. Only he had the fortune of peeping into his other sides; for instance, his eternally genuine courage and complete devotion.

How he could always haul Ye Qin out from the dark abyss and bring him on top of the clouds to look at the beauty of this world. How he could evoke Ye Qin's best, most beautiful imagination of the future and happiness.

Of course he couldn't not agree.

He lifted the hand that Cheng Feichi kissed and kissed his hand as well. "Yes," he said, very soft but very clear.

Flowers were scattered as everyone clapped.

For quite a few days, Ye Qin lost himself in this belated wedding. When he suddenly realized he had taken the place of the bride, he immediately jumped up.

"I should have proposed!" he said frantically. "I gave you the ring. I should be the groom!"

When Cheng Feichi heard this, he silently took out a pair of men's rings that had been prepared but never prompted from

his pocket.

"I don't care! I gave you the ring first!" Ye Qin refused to accept.

Cheng Feichi just smiled, as if he was telling him, *As long as you're happy.*

Of course one could never have too many rings. The next day, Ye Qin went to work wearing both.

One on his left hand, one on his right, both on the ring finger.

When asked by reporters, Ye Qin showed them off very proudly. "I proposed once, he proposed once. Doesn't that make two rings?"

As soon as he turned, it was written into a press release: *Formerly Invisible Idol Flaunts Ring after Marrying into Money.*

"I was making a public display of affection, okay?" Ye Qin scoffed at this.

"Okay." Cheng Feichi nodded.

Ye Qin then thought of something. "You left something out at our wedding ceremony."

Cheng Feichi looked at him with a tilt of his head. "What did I leave out?"

"From now on, you'll be beside me, trust me, depend on me, and..." Ye Qin leaned into his ear and finished somewhat bashfully, "...love me."

Cheng Feichi froze at first, then said, "You know that."

"Of course I do." Ye Qin curled his lip. "But I still want to hear you say it."

Cheng Feichi knew he was finding things to pick at, but he remained helpless to Ye Qin's coquettish act.

And so, Ye Qin succeeded in hearing his first solemn, "I love you."

Having gotten an inch, he demanded a mile. "Say it again."

Unbothered, Cheng Feichi repeated, "I love you."

"Again."

"I love you."

"Again! Again!"

"I love you."

Ye Qin listened until he felt as clouded and intoxicated as if he were drunk. Finally, he switched to another question, "Who am I?"

Long, slender fingers slid through black hair at the back of his head. With a single hand, Cheng Feichi propped up Ye Qin's nape and pushed forward, easily touching that pair of soft lips.

"Ye Qin, Ye Xiaoruan, my baby," Cheng Feichi called him, so close they seemed to fuse together.

His voice was low and hoarse, like he was also completely absorbed, unable to break free henceforth.

In short, Ye Qin was very satisfied with this wedding ceremony, so satisfied that he had to take out the live recording and review it every day.

As for how the marketing accounts spreading rumors and wreaking havoc were all rounded up and brought to court and then made it onto trending, that was a story for another time.

EXTRA 08

Ye Qin—Those Five Years Without You

THE first year.

Mother was gone. Father wasn't around either. All that remained was me and what felt like a lifetime of debt I could never repay.

The day I received my acceptance letter, I went to Cheng Fei-chi's building and looked up at the window that never lit up again.

If he knew I'd been accepted into the school we had promised to attend together, would he be happy? Would he smile at me?

Back in my dormitory that night, I kept the acceptance letter in the bottommost drawer in a futile attempt at denial—if I couldn't see it, I could pretend it never came.

But when I closed the drawer, the fear returned, the fear that I might, over time, come to believe his existence was a dream too, ephemeral and elusive.

At the book signing last week, a fan saw the ring on my finger and posted about it online. The company told me to stop wearing the ring to avoid unwanted speculation.

But I had to keep it with me. I *needed* to. So I found a string and threaded it through the ring to wear around my neck.

Only when I touched this ring could I be sure he had been

here before.

He *was* here. I'm sure of that.

The second year.

Like a bird with clipped wings, I floundered and struggled to get by in the entertainment industry.

I stumbled a lot, but I also learned many hard truths, especially how hard it was to make money.

Someone from the dorm moved out to live alone, and Song Xu asked me if I wanted to co-rent with him. I did the math. Moving out would increase my monthly expenses by at least three thousand; it wasn't worth it.

It reminded me of the time Cheng Feichi was training in the suburbs. I asked him to live with me, and he even made a show of paying me rent despite already having a dorm to stay in. That was such an unnecessary expense...but he thought it was worth it. Would he regret that decision now?

I sighed, losing myself in these memories. As I turned over on the narrow bed, I felt something wet slide down my cheeks, and that was when I realized I was crying.

The third year.

Truth be told, I don't really like being an artist, but whenever I checked my private messages in my free time and saw so many strangers showing me their support and love, I felt like I couldn't slack off; I had to pull myself together.

The group didn't officially disband, but its members went their separate ways and pursued solo careers, leaving Song Xu and me as the only regular residents of the dorm.

Never in my wildest dreams would I imagine I'd one day be cooking for myself.

Song Xu was a young man with a big appetite, so I always

gave him a big portion of the food. He gobbled it down and complimented me on my cooking.

"That's because you've never tasted real cooking before," I replied.

That night, I dreamed *he* cooked up a feast for me. I tried to reach for the food, but somehow, I just couldn't move.

And so, my bucket list grew by one more wish: to taste Cheng Feichi's cooking again.

I'd finish it all and lick the plate clean, then shower him with praises, hugs, and kisses.

Just once—that was all I asked.

The fourth year.

I called Wei Jiaqi again at the start of the new year, even though I knew the answer would be "still no news."

I paid off most of the debt and started taking on gigs that others might consider beneath me—all for the sake of money. This time, it was a real estate ad that was supposed to run on public transport.

Oh, the irony. Here I was, a person deep in debt with no car or house to my name, advertising real estate.

I wonder if he'd see it.

That thought was even more hilarious; he was in America, how could he possibly see it? And even if he were to chance upon it, he'd probably pretend not to recognize me and walk away.

After the shoot was done, I played with some free Lego sets in the studio lounge and built a house. Not too big, not too small. Just right for two people. But then I remembered he probably wouldn't want to live with me anymore.

Didn't matter. I'll move in all the Lego Technic sets he built for me and buy even more Legos. That way, I wouldn't be as lonely living alone...maybe.

The fifth year.

The company organized a small birthday party for me at the end of the year.

When it was time to blow the candles, Song Xu tried to get me to reveal my wish, but I was afraid it wouldn't come true if I did, so I turned him down.

Having drunk a bit, I was feeling tipsy when I got into the cab, and it was only after arriving at the destination that I realized it was the airport.

The driver noticed me staring blankly at the airport and asked if I wanted to go back, but I said no, paid the fare, and got out.

No matter the hour, the airport was always bustling with activity. I stood in the emptiest spot in the plaza and watched as the people came and went, feeling utterly lost.

Ever since that day I rushed here only to miss him, I have never stayed more than necessary.

As if on cue, it began to rain. I looked up at the gloomy sky above, thinking I could finally let my tears flow. No tears came, however, and the rain pattered down, each drop stabbing like blades into my heart.

It hurt so much, and still, I couldn't cry. Because growing up made me understand tears were the most worthless thing of all.

Instead, I let my mind run loose with thoughts of him—his smile, his virtues, and the view of his departing figure as he left without looking back.

I came down with a fever when I returned home. Song Xu said I kept calling for him in my sleep. "I didn't know you had a brother."

"I do," I replied, "but I did something wrong and made him angry, and now he doesn't want to see me."

"Then so be it," Song Xu said casually. "It's not like you need him to survive."

I paused for a moment, taken aback, then I shook my head. "But I miss him."

I missed him. So, so much. So much more than I wanted to repay my debt or buy a house.

If he didn't miss me, I'll miss him enough for both of us.

Then maybe he wouldn't be mad anymore.

And maybe he'll come back sooner.

EXTRA 09

About Them

- **Double 11 Single's Day [Chinese Black Friday]**

First of all, our industrious and thrifty Ye Xiaoruan was definitely participating.

Ye Qin thought to himself, *50 yuan off for 400 yuan spent, 20 yuan off for 200 yuan spent. Plus the stackable coupon from the store that gives 100 yuan off 400. I'm still short of 28.36 to hit 400. Let me ask the class monitor if there's anything he wants to buy... Oh, wait, the Sunrise duty-free shop has an extra 30% off...*

Ye Qin gave up after calculating for a while.

Ugh. Forget it. I might as well ask Ning Lan from the other group. He's a math whiz!

Ning Lan came online.

Ning Lan: *[It's simple. Look, the discount of 100 off a purchase of 400 isn't all that good. The shop has a discount of 500 if you buy 1000 yuan worth of items, and there is an additional 20% off during the first hour. Why don't we pool our orders and split the cost later?]*

Sui Yi: *[Baby, I'm not all that broke...]*

Ning Lan: *[Well, a penny saved is a penny earned.]*

Ye Qin: *[*clings* Yes, yes, right! Whatever you say! We're*

gonna save big this time!]

Cheng Feichi could only watch from the sidelines in silence.

Zhou Jinheng then created a group chat. Besides himself, the members included his "Wife," "Bro-in-law," and "Sis-in-law," as per his aliases for them.

Yi Hui: *[Bro- and sis-in-law, please help me with this discount event! *pleading eyes*]*

Ye Qin: *[Gege, and that what's-his-name dude, click this link for me!]*

Yi Hui: *[Yes! And that what's-his-name as well! Help me out too!]*

Zhou Jinheng: *[??? Me?]*

Ye Qin: *[Gege, gege, your work acc hasn't clicked yet, right? Gimme a boost!]*

Yi Hui: *[Bro, me too! *doe eyes*]*

Ye Qin: *[What's-your-name, do you have any other accounts?]*

Yi Hui: *[Do you? Do you? *starry eyes*]*

Zhou What's-His-Name Speechless.

Ye Qin and Yi Hui weren't on the same team, but after spamming links to beg for clicks every day, they would summarize the day's progress and encourage (read: compete against) each other.

Zhou Jinheng didn't participate, but he didn't want to see Yi Hui lose, so he would secretly buy clicks for him every day right before the cutoff time.

Zhou Jinheng: *[My wife's gotta win!]*

Zhou Jinheng even slid into Cheng Feichi's private messages.

Zhou Jinheng: *[Wanna buy clicks?]*

Cheng Feichi: *[Nah, you guys have fun.]*

But then he turned around and gifted Ye Qin a red packet, doing whatever little he could help.

Ye Qin: *[Why send me a red packet out of the blue? Wait—quick! Check the group chat and click on that link for a coupon exchange for me! I need ten clicks!]*

Cheng Feichi was speechless.

Meanwhile, Ji Zhinan, a recent advocate for health wellness, believed that no face mask was as effective as going to bed early.

He added everything he wanted to buy to his shopping cart a day before. Too cool (read: lazy) to participate in the event or red-packet sharing activities, he simply clicked on the "one-click checkout" at the designated time and went to bed early with his hubby in his arms.

But when he woke up, he realized he'd selected the wrong address and had everything sent to Qin Weiyu's company, with "Little Star's Tiny Universe" jotted down in the name column.

Worse still, they'd already been shipped. There was no turning back now.

Ji Zhinan buried his face in his hands, wondering just how in the world he was going to explain this embarrassing nickname to Qin Weiyu.

- **Another Double 11 Single's Day**

Ye Qin bought a shirt and left a review:

It's a perfect fit. My gege looks so ridiculously handsome in it. He's the most handsome guy in the universe. Not showing any pics though. You guys just have to use your imagination.

- **And Yet Another Double 11 Single's Day**

Our dear Qin-Qin didn't deign himself to participate in our peasant shopping spree this year. At the time of the shop-

ping frenzy, he was already fast asleep in bed, cuddling with his bed-warmer Cheng Feichi and murmuring in his sleep about how delicious the breakfast today was and how aromatic the milk smelled.

Resigned, Cheng Feichi freed a hand and took out his phone to search for "QQ Star Children's Growth Milk" on a certain orange app.

• **Test of Love**

Around the Qixi Festival—also known as Chinese Valentine's Day—four teams of celebrity guests on a reality show underwent a test of love the production team had "thoughtfully" designed.

Ye Qin, the guest for the episode after this one, expressed his bafflement upon hearing about this. "Are you sure this is a Qixi special and not a ploy to break up as many couples as possible?"

The director waved his hand dismissively. "Of course not. In fact, a few couples have heaped praise on this segment for strengthening their bonds!"

Ye Qin was skeptical, but this was a punishment he had to take after failing a game that afternoon. He was on tenterhooks as he stared at his phone, silently praying Cheng Feichi would be too busy at work tonight to call him. 

It didn't go the way he hoped. The call came in at 8 p.m. sharp.

Already on edge, his heart leaped into his throat when he heard the actress's saccharine, "Hellooo." 

"Please put Ye Qin on the phone," Cheng Feichi said.

"Ohhh, he's in the shower." The actress followed the script. "Would you like me to pass him a message?"

"Still at work?" Cheng Feichi asked.

"Ohhh no, we got done ages ago. But he had a craving for something sweet and said he's gonna buy me some candies later."

Ye Qin was speechless. *She's really done her homework; she even knows my tastes.*

He thought Cheng Feichi would start to get suspicious by now. But after a moment of silence, Cheng Feichi said, "Well, then, please remind him to drink his milk before going to bed."

The actress was dumbstruck.

"Also, tell him to put on more clothing tomorrow. It'll be cold."

"...Sure," the actress replied after a moment's silence.

"And call me when filming wraps up. I'll pick him up."

"...That's all?"

"Oh yeah," Cheng Feichi replied in a calm tone. "Tell him not to eat too many candies outside; we still have a lot at home."

When the episode was aired, Ye Qin and Cheng Feichi watched it together.

Mortified by his flustered look on screen, Ye Qin wished he could crawl into a hole. He scrambled to find the remote control to change the channel, but couldn't find it anywhere.

"You knew this was part of the show all along, right?" Ye Qin huffed. "You were sure I wouldn't dare to cheat on you."

Cheng Feichi said nothing and just smiled as he unwrapped a piece of candy.

Ye Qin's anger evaporated in an instant. He grasped Cheng Feichi's hand and leaned in to eat the candy, his cheeks full as he said, "The candy at home is still the sweetest... You're super sweet."

"Not me. *You* are the candy," Cheng Feichi said.

Ye Qin cocked his head. "What about you then?"

Cheng Feichi glanced at the wrapper in his hand. "I'm the wrapper."

A once-blank piece of paper that, after embracing the candy, was now a vibrant hue of colors from being coated in its sweetness.

- **First Day of School**

Today, Ye Qin reported for the first day of the school year.
Cheng Feichi took time out of his busy schedule to send him a
text. *[Send me your class schedule.]*

Ye Qin: *[Why? /puzzled]*

Cheng Feichi: *[Supervising you.]*

Ye Qin: *[There's no need for that! I'm already so old now /wipes
sweat]*

Cheng Feichi: *[I'm going to buy you some study guides.]*

Ye Qin: *[!!! I don't want them /grips hair]*

Cheng Feichi: *[Just in case you fail your subjects again this
semester.]*

Ye Qin: *[...How did you find out?]*

Cheng Feichi: *[Your teacher sent me an email at the end of
last semester.]*

Ye Qin: *[!!! Which teacher?]*

Cheng Feichi: *[Basic Theory of Performing]*

Ye Qin: *[I knew it! He's got too much free time!]*

Cheng Feichi: *[And University-Level English too.]*

Ye Qin: *[......]*

Cheng Feichi: *[Two subjects.]*

Ye Qin: *[/collapse]*

Cheng Feichi: *[You failed both.]*

Ye Qin: *[I only needed a little more to pass /pitiful]*

Cheng Feichi: *[You'll do the make-up exams next week.]*

Ye Qin: *[/goes mad]*

Ye Qin: *[Hold on, do the teachers know you're my...that?]*

Cheng Feichi: *[I said I'm your parent.]*

Ye Qin: *[......]*

Cheng Feichi: *[Your class schedule.]*

Ye Qin: *[Gege...... /pitiful /about to cry]*

Cheng Feichi: *[Your class schedule.]*

Ye Qin: *[Class schedule.jpg]*

Ye Qin: *[/wails /wails /wails]*

Cheng Feichi: *[I'll make you sweet and sour pork ribs tonight.]*

Ye Qin: *[I love you gege /rose]*

Cheng Feichi: *[After you memorize the key points for your subjects.]*

Ye Qin: *[/wither /wither /wither]*

From that moment on, it was as though the student Ye Xiaoruan had returned to high school, living a blissful life where he had someone making sure he was following up on his studies.

- **About Them**

Things You Might Not Know About Them

1.

Cheng Feichi can take spicy food, at the level where he's able to eat spicy peppers raw without any change in his expression.

Ye Qin can't. One time his sense of competitiveness welled up within him, and he insisted on competing with Cheng Feichi over this no matter how much he tried to dissuade him. When he was first eating the peppers, it was fine, but when the spiciness kicked in, it felt like he was expelling flames from both his mouth and nose. After drinking eight cups of water and spending the entire night in the bathroom, he didn't dare to do it again.

2.

There was another reason why Ye Qin didn't dare to eat spicy food, and that was because he would get pimples afterwards. They'd appear either on his forehead or his chin, and when they popped up, he couldn't resist poking at them. Being rather vain, he also didn't want to leave any scars, and so he suffered each time this happened.

Cheng Feichi didn't rely on his face for his work, and he also never got pimples. Ye Qin was extremely jealous, and there was a period, when he was dieting, that he would prepare hotpot every day and make Cheng Feichi eat it in front of him, saying that he would be able to satiate his desires by just watching the pot.

Cheng Feichi asked, "I'm the pot?"

Ye Qin confirmed, "You're a handsome pot, a handy, handy handsome pot."

#Tears of Time#

3.

Very few people knew that Ye Qin had quite decent grades before high school. He was slightly above the class average, but when he was in his third year of middle school, he started to hit a wall, and after facing those barriers for some time, he just gave up and stopped studying entirely.

Despite that, during his high school entrance examination, he still managed scores of above 130 for mathematics and physics.

As for chemistry, he only scored 25 points.

Whereas for Cheng Feichi, ever since he started attending school, he had never left the treasured number one spot, not even in kindergarten.

#The Experience of Dating a Top Student#

Ye Qin: *[Thanks for the ask. Occasionally, it feels embarrassing, but most of the time, it feels pretty awesome.]*

4.

Ye Qin had always thought Cheng Feichi's good figure came naturally to him. He only found out later on that there was a gym in his company building. During noon, if he wasn't working, he would go there to run and lift, and he had a set of workout clothes stored there specifically.

Upon hearing about this, Ye Qin's first reaction was to ask, "Is this gym public or private?"

Cheng Feichi replied, "It's private."

Ye Qin heaved a sigh of relief.

Cheng Feichi asked, "What if it's public?"

"I'll immediately get people to cover all the glass windows there, then I'll change the door lock to a fingerprint one, and only my fingerprint will be able to open the door."

#The Experience of Having a Partner Who Easily Gets Jealous#

Cheng Feichi: *[Thanks for the ask. It's not too bad, just that I can't go to the gym anymore.]*

Ye Qin: *[Why do you have to lift weights? Just lift me!]*

5.

When Ye Qin was young, he had two years of piano lessons, and he even participated in a youth performance held by the Children's Center in the city. A rather blurry video of the performance existed, and when he just debuted, his company even used it to build up his image as having grown up in a rich family.

Cheng Feichi had watched the video before. One of the employees in his company had sent it to him.

The little Ye Qin in the video seemed around the age of eight or nine. He was dressed in a suit, and he even had a bow tie. Sitting on the piano stool, his back was ramrod straight, and he did look rather like a professional pianist.

Ye Qin was very embarrassed. "Wasn't my playing awful?"

"No, it sounded very good."

"Don't tease me. Out of the 365 days that I spent learning to play the piano, I was goofing off for 360."

"Little children are all playful."

Ye Qin perked up in interest. "What were you doing around that age?"

He was asking about Cheng Feichi's interests. During those years, every parent had high hopes for their child, and most of them would make their children learn something outside of school.

In actual fact, Cheng Feichi did attend drawing classes as a child. Drawing could sharpen one's patience, and Cheng Feichi was also interested in it, so he was willing to learn.

Later on, Cheng Xin's health deteriorated, and thus Cheng Feichi took the initiative to give up his lessons. After school, he would go home to take care of his mother, helping to take up the responsibility of housework. He was so busy that he had no time to think about any of his interests.

He didn't want Ye Qin to be sad, and so he said, "Listening to you play the piano."

• A Plain and Unremarkable Handsome Man

Everyone knew that Ye Qin was a person full of contradictions. This was embodied in how, whenever he had time, he would go around bragging, afraid that people didn't know he had an outstanding husband. However, he didn't allow others to have even the slightest trace of covetousness; only envy.

As such, during an interview with a magazine, when he was asked what sort of person Mr. Cheng was, Ye Qin was torn for quite some time before he finally answered, "A plain and unremarkable handsome man."

The reporter was speechless. "..."

• Name Change

It was another year, and Ye Qin could finally change his name again on Weibo.

Being a public figure, he didn't dare make changes to his

main account, but he could change his alternate account; no one would know, anyway.

Ye Qin got up early, brimming with excitement, and changed his name from *Your Friendly Neighborhood Ironman* to *Cheng Feichi Global Fan Club*.

He then privately messaged Cheng Feichi's dormant Weibo account: *[Hello~ I'm the president of your fan club (づ>/////<)づ♡]*

Cheng Feichi: *[dot]*

Fan Club: *[Do you like me? (≧∪≦)]*

Cheng Feichi: *[I like Ye Qin]*

- **Fair Complexion**

Come summer, a magazine interviewed four male celebrities voted as having the best skin in the entertainment industry and asked them how they maintained such radiant complexions year after year.

Ye Qin (born 1996.11.29) looked vexed upon hearing this question. He had no skincare experience and didn't want to lie to everyone, but he also didn't want to look dismissive by not answering. After struggling for a long time, he decided to tell the truth. "Uh…It's n-natural."

Meanwhile, off-camera, the staff distributed questionnaires to each of the four celebrities' partners. Who knew, maybe some of their responses might be featured in a new section of the magazine.

The questions were quite standard, ranging from their partners' favorite colors to how they met, how long they had been together to their most memorable date, an unforgettable gift they had received, and so on—basically the kind of content the public was curious about.

Cheng Feichi (born 1994.02.13) didn't even think twice as he gave his answer for "most memorable date"—watching a mara-

thon of *Spider-Man: Far From Home* five times in a single day.

- **Birthday Wish**

Ye Qin's birthday wish this year was to hear Cheng Feichi sing.

Cheng Feichi found this request a little hard to fulfill and asked him to choose another, but Ye Qin insisted.

His wait began early in the morning, when he played *Right Here Waiting* by Richard Marx on the speakers during breakfast and hummed the chorus when sending Cheng Feichi to work. A lunchtime, he sighed dramatically over the phone, "A birthday without singing is like sweet and sour pork ribs without the sugar. How meaningless."

Cheng Feichi didn't know what to say to that.

Even later that evening, as Ye Qin was blowing out the candles at home, he still looked forlorn. "If not, you can just sing happy birthday; that would be good enough for me too."

And finally, as they nestled in bed that night, Cheng Feichi sang.

Other than *Happy Birthday*, he also sang *Kiss You* by One Direction.

His ears turning bright red, Ye Qin shyly pulled the covers over his head and asked in a small voice, "Who is this 'you' you're kissing?"

"Ye Qin," Cheng Feichi obligingly breathed in his ear.

- **I'm Home**

A-Ruan: *[I'm home, wifey]*
Cfc: *[ok]*
A-Ruan: *[damn! my hand slipped!]*
Cfc: *[slipped?]*

A-Ruan: *[damn auto-correct]*

A-Ruan: *[I turned it off!]*

A-Ruan: *[I turned it on again!]*

A-Ruan: *[If I repeat it enough, it'll get used to it!]*

A-Ruan: *[I'm home honey honey honey]*

A-Ruan: *[I'm home hubby hubby hubby]*

A-Ruan: *[don't ignore me (pleading eyes)]*

Cfc: *[I'm not ignoring you. Go to bed early if you're home. I'll be back tomorrow.]*

A-Ruan: *[oh honey hubby I love you ♥]*

- **Mirror, Mirror, On The Wall, Who Has The Fairest Legs Of 'Em All**

Ning Lan and Sui Yi had a strawberry field in their courtyard.

Ye Qin met Ning Lan at a commercial performance and hit it off with him. Finding himself with some free time recently, he decided to visit Ning Lan and pick strawberries—and compare whose legs were more like those from girl groups.

Ning Lan: *[I have the best legs in my group!]*

Ye Qin: *[So do I.]*

Ning Lan: *[But your group flopped.]*

Ye Qin: *[凸(⁺⁺Ⅲ⁺⁺)]*

Ye Qin: *[My merc sells out in seconds, okay?]*

Ning Lan: *[Yeah, all bought by that simp of yours. Meanwhile, people can't even get their hands on my man's merc.]*

Ye Qin: *[You look awfully happy for someone who has to deal with so many people lusting after your guy.]*

Ning Lan had no comeback to that.

That evening, when Sui Yi returned home, Ning Lan gave him the cold shoulder.

Sui Yi called Ye Qin up.

Sui Yi: *[It's not very nice of you to sow discord between us after eating and taking our strawberries, isn't it?]*

Ye Qin: *[Hahahahahahaha, that's what you get for causing us to flop.]*

After hanging up, Sui Yi said to Ning Lan, "Baby, you see. We're a group. We need to stick together."

Ning Lan asked, "What group? I quit a long time ago, remember?"

"We're family, too," said Sui Yi.

"Since when?" asked Ning Lan.

Unable to win the argument, Sui Yi took out the household register and slapped it on the table.

Ning Lan leaned in for a look and made an interested noise. "Ohhhhh…"

"Hm?"

"So your name really is Sui Yi," commented Ning Lan.

"What else would it be?" asked Sui Yi.

Ning Lan wrapped his arms around Sui Yi's neck and breathed into his ear. "Hubby~"

The next day, Ye Qin couldn't take it lying down when he learned that his friends didn't quarrel, but instead spent a (s)exciting night together.

When Cheng Feichi returned home that night, Ye Qin did the same and slapped his household register on the table.

"Thinking of a divorce?" asked Cheng Feichi.

Ye Qin was shocked. "Wait, what? This isn't how it's supposed to go. Quick, ask me for my name."

Cheng Feichi stated, "Ye Qin."

"No, look at my title in the household register," said Ye Qin.

Cheng Feichi stated, "Head of household."

"No, look again," said Ye Qin. "Someone's legal spouse."

Cheng Feichi confirmed, "Uh-huh."

Ye Qin was confused: "Huh...?"

Cheng Feichi clarified: My wife.

Ye Qin was delighted. /(//·/w/·//)/ Hehhehheheheh~

After a (s)exciting night, Cheng Feichi asked, "Still want a divorce?"

Ye Qin declared, "No! Never! Even if the sky falls, I will never, never, never, ever leave you!"

With nothing else to do the next day, Ye Qin lay in bed and called Ning Lan.

Ye Qin: *[Ugh, my waist is killing me. I'm not going today.]*

Ning Lan: *[Ugh, my ass is killing me. I can't entertain you either.]*

Ye Qin: *[Damn, just how bad is Sui Yi's technique?]*

Ning Lan was speechless.

• A Little Snippet of Daily Life

Cheng Feichi was occasionally slow on the uptake, while Ye Qin typically had the memory of a goldfish. So it was common for Ye Qin to tell Cheng Feichi a joke, only to burst into laughter even before finishing it, while Cheng Feichi remained unmoved.

With surprise, Ye Qin asked, "Isn't it funny?"

Cheng Feichi said calmly, "It is."

Even more surprised, Ye Qin asked, "Then why aren't you laughing?"

Cheng Feichi gave a calm laugh. "Ha ha ha."

Ye Qin was speechless.

But the next night, as both of them were turning in for the night, Cheng Feichi suddenly laughed.

"What's so funny?" Ye Qin asked.

"I just thought of the joke you told me yesterday," Replied Cheng Feichi.

"Huh? What joke?"

Cheng Feichi calmly repeated the joke.

"Oh, that one!" Ye Qin exclaimed, before laughing hysterically for the next five minutes. "Haha!"

EXTRA 10

Christmas Eve

THE night of Christmas Eve.

Ye Qin received a Spider-Man figure, and excitedly, he asked Cheng Feichi, "How did you know I like Speederman?"

Mr. Cheng corrected his pronunciation. "It's 'spider,' not 'speeder.'"

Ye Qin blinked. "Then what does 'speeder' mean?"

"Something or someone that goes very fast."

"It's about the same, about the same." Ye Qin waved him off unconcernedly. "Speederman's really fast. Pew, pew, pew!"

Cheng Feichi was speechless. "..."

The next day, Ye Qin woke up very early. After running about everywhere, he finally managed to buy a small acrylic box.

On the way to the live broadcasting studio, he sat in the passenger seat, manipulating that Spider-Man figure. Placing it in the box, Ye Qin took it out again, and no matter how he looked at it, he felt that it just didn't look right. On a whim, he wanted to drill a hole into the box and thread a string through it.

"Isn't it nice enough like this?" asked Cheng Feichi.

"It doesn't work." Ye Qin had a look of distress on his face,

and he placed the Spider-Man figure in the box on the console. "Like this, Spider-Man is crouching down. He doesn't look cool at all."

Cheng Feichi was speechless. "..."

He should have bought him the Spider-Man in the climbing pose, and not the hanging one.

When they arrived at their destination, it was extremely crowded. Fans had completely overwhelmed the entrance such that no one could enter.

Cheng Feichi escorted Ye Qin to the backdoor, and they were surprised by a couple kissing in a corner there.

The kiss ended. Sui Yi still had his arms around Ning Lan's waist, and he leaned into his ear. "Go ahead, I'll be waiting for you here."

Ning Lan pushed him a foot away, still keeping his hands on Sui Yi's shoulders. "Aren't you going to be Father Christmas for your fans today?"

"That's at night, and it'll just be for a short while." It was rare that Sui Yi saw Ning Lan get jealous, and he was internally delighted. "Come with me. Father Christmas will give you a present."

Ning Lan clicked his tongue. "I don't want a present that everyone has."

"Then, what would you like?"

Sui Yi watched him leave. In less than two minutes, his phone vibrated. Ning Lan had sent him a text. *[Not Father.]*

Sui Yi did not understand. *[Huh?]*

Ning Lan texted: *[You're the world's stupidest Father Christmas.]*

Sui Yi was speechless. "..."

Many celebrities had been invited for the broadcast today,

both famous or not, both past and present. All sorts of celebrities were present, and there was something for both the old and young audience watching.

One of the biggest celebrities there was the A-list actor Ji Zhinan, and the people gathering at the entrance, holding up posters of stars made with LED lights, were all his fans.

However, he didn't seem very happy. Standing backstage, he was holding his phone, and he looked to be waiting for someone.

Seeing that the broadcast was about to start, he couldn't help but send a text. *[Are you still coming? /angry]*

Qin Weiyu replied after a while. *[I'm sorry, work came up suddenly /about to cry]*

Crestfallen, blood rushed to Ji Zhinan's head from anger. *[Don't act cute! /dagger]*

Qin Weiyu: *[OK /aggrieved]*

Ji Zhinan: *[You'll be sleeping in the study tonight! /explosion]*

Qin Weiyu stopped sending emoticons, abruptly turning solemn. *[That won't do.]*

Backstage, in the lounge for friends and family.

Using his car key, Cheng Feichi was creating a small hole in the acrylic box. After spending quite some time on it, he had only made a tiny dent.

Qin Weiyu had been sitting there and watching him for a while, and he said, "If you want to make a hole, you might need a drill."

The two people had interacted at work before, and so they knew each other. Cheng Feichi smiled. "I'm only giving it a try. I don't want him to be too anxious from waiting."

From the other side of the room, despite how busy he was, Sui Yi looked up. "When I came in through the backdoor, I saw that there was a drill in the venue's toolbox. We can borrow it

from them."

He then went back to staring at the words "Father Christmas" written on a piece of paper.

Cheng Feichi managed to borrow the drill, and with Qin Weiyu's aid, he pierced a hole in the box.

"Thank you. I've never used a drill before, I couldn't have done it without you," Cheng Feichi expressed his gratitude sincerely.

Company President Qin, who often built little things like kennels and star lamps at home for his spouse, said modestly, "It's nothing, you don't have to stand on such courtesy."

Cheng Feichi looked over at the starry gift box, big enough for a person to stand inside, that was in the corner of the lounge. He asked, "Was that made by you?"

Qin Weiyu nodded. "In the past, it was him who always gave me surprises. This time, I'll be the one giving it to him."

Cheng Feichi said, "Mr. Qin is very thoughtful."

Qin Weiyu looked at the little box in Cheng Feichi's hands. "Mr. Cheng, as well."

Over here, the two company presidents were each praising the other politely, while over there, Sui Yi suddenly leapt to his feet, holding the A4 paper up.

He finally understood. Not 'father'? Then could it be 'husband'?

The man, younger than his partner, grinned like a fool at his piece of paper, while the other two men, older than their partners, looked at him in disdain.

You'll never understand what it's like to be called "gege."

EXTRA 11

Valentine's Day

EARLIER in the year, Ye Qin had agreed to appear on an escape room variety show.

"Never fight a battle unprepared" had been his recent mantra. Armed with an attitude of wanting to learn, he brought Cheng Feichi to play at all the various escape room games available nearby. Although all the riddles were pretty much solved by Cheng Feichi, Ye Qin still felt a great sense of achievement. The night before the filming of the show, he blabbed about how he would definitely be the first player to escape the room on his social media. The next day, when he was on the way to the filming, he started to get nervous. Repeatedly, he confirmed that Cheng Feichi's phone was fully charged, and that he had enough talk time on his plan.

"If—I'm saying, if—I get stuck on a rather difficult stage and call you, don't answer too quickly..." instructed Ye Qin solemnly. "We can't let people see that you're specially waiting for my call."

Cheng Feichi nodded in agreement. "Sure."

Before getting out of the car, Ye Qin then added anxiously, "But you can't answer too slowly either. Let the phone ring about four or five times, that's perfect."

Cheng Feichi agreed again, leaning over and helping Ye Qin undo his seat belt. Taking the opportunity, he gave Ye Qin a peck on his fair, tender cheek, and Ye Qin's eyes rounded in shock. His eyes darted around, eyeing their surroundings before abruptly remembering that they had just publicly announced their marriage earlier in the year. Momentarily, he felt that he had just been taken advantage of, and so he decisively leaned over, lunging onto Cheng Feichi in his driver seat, smacking a kiss right onto his lips.

Cheng Feichi was already used to dealing with his sudden attacks, and thus he allowed the younger man to hold him down, lifting his arm and wrapping it around his waist to prevent him from feeling uncomfortable in this position, while his other hand slid around the back of his head as he deepened the kiss.

After a duel between tongues, Ye Qin collapsed back into his seat, gasping. He panted as he said, "Th-the last time, when we saw that someone and his someone else doing that outside the studio, I felt like that was too much. Now..."

"Now?" asked Cheng Feichi.

Ye Qin grinned. "Now, I only want to be with gege every minute and every second of the day."

In the studio, after his makeup was done, Ye Qin bumped into that "someone" who had just hurried over. Surprised, Ye Qin wondered why the production crew didn't mention anything about the change in guests.

The other party came up and greeted him. "Good morning, Senior."

Ye Qin had been in this industry for quite a number of years, and only in recent times did he finally become a little more popular. For someone to refer to him as a senior, he was a little shy. Still, strictly speaking, Ning Lan was his junior. Ye Qin,

who loved to protect his dignity and always felt that he had to live up to his reputation, thus responded with as much aloofness as possible.

"Good morning. You're here for the show as well?"

Ning Lan was actually two years older than him, but he had a baby face. When he smiled, two sweet dimples popped out, and the tiny mole at the corner of his eye further embellished the liveliness and vividness of them. Just one glance was enough to see that he was the sort to be very popular with the audience, and it was no wonder despite having quit the entertainment industry, he still received many invitations from various popular shows.

"I guess so," answered Ning Lan with a laugh. "I'm here as a reserve player. But the guests invited today are all famous for their intelligence, and there's a chance I wouldn't have a chance to appear throughout the entire show."

Ye Qin took his words as a compliment for himself, feeling rather pleased about it. When the recording started, even if he drew an escape room with a difficulty rating of 5 stars, he was still full of confidence.

Only when he finally entered the first room, which was the legendary stage known for basically giving out points for free, and the guest he was partnered with still standing there in a daze after the riddle was solved, Ye Qin suddenly had a premonition that he might not succeed.

"So it's actually like this. You're really smart." His partner, Ji Zhinan, upon hearing how he came to the riddle's solution, patted him on the shoulder with a smile. "I normally don't like to play games that require so much brain power. When I accepted the show's invitation, I had to confirm many times that they didn't invite the wrong person. Now that you're here, I'm no longer worried."

Ye Qin and Ji Zhinan could be considered to have debuted

around the same time. However, the other person was an A-list actor who had clinched a Best Actor title before, while he was only a D-list actor whose career had perked up slightly in recent times. Ye Qin gave a few dry coughs, feigning steadiness as he said, "I'll try my best."

He didn't expect that everything would crumble when they entered their second room.

In the vast, empty room was a guzheng, a Chinese plucked zither. The speakers were playing a loop of a folk music segment, and it seemed like the key to unlocking this room was to play the segment on the guzheng.

Ye Qin had pretty much only switched to becoming a singer as an adult, and he had never gone through a proper study of music. Even reading music took a lot of effort for him, and for him to play on the guzheng was basically impossible. Instead, it was Ji Zhinan who listened carefully to the melody playing before walking over to the guzheng and plucking at a few strings. In a few short moments, he was able to smoothly play the segment of the folk melody.

This time, it was Ye Qin's turn to express his admiration. Unconcernedly, Ji Zhinan smiled. "I learned the piano as a child, and I just happen to have this ability. If you learned it before, you would be able to do so too."

Up until now, the game was progressing quite harmoniously. However, when they entered the third room, while Ye Qin was searching for the light switch in the dark, he heard a commotion. By the time the lights turned on, Ji Zhinan had already been trapped in the metal cage in the middle of the room.

After trying methods like squeezing between the bars of the cage, shifting the cage, and using pliers to break the bars, all to no avail, Ji Zhinan gripped the bars from inside with both

hands, sticking his head between them. Not knowing whether to laugh or cry, he said, "At this moment, should I be singing *Tears Behind Bars?*"

Ye Qin smacked himself on the head. "Right! We can request for help from outside!"

According to the rules of the show, each time a lifeline was used, a guest would have to be eliminated. Ji Zhinan took the first "sacrifice" and made the call. While waiting, he continuously assured Ye Qin that his helper outside was very clever, and they would definitely know what to do.

Ye Qin thought, *My gege is very clever too. Later on, when it's my turn to ask for help, everyone will definitely be shocked.*

The call connected, and the person answering was a man. "Hello? Xiao-Xing?"

Ji Zhinan's face was all puckered up. "I've been trapped in a cage, and I can't get out."

From the change in Ji Zhinan's tone and attitude, onlooker Ye Qin keenly perceived who was the person who answered. Silently, he retreated a couple of steps, not listening, not watching, and not being a third wheel.

Having heard Ji Zhinan describe the situation onsite, the person on the other end of the call remained silent for a moment before saying, "Following along the roof of the cage, are you able to find the source of the rope?"

His words were a reminder for Ye Qin. He looked upwards towards the wiring of the ceiling before striding over to a corner of the room and smacking the switch on the wall.

In the end, not only did nothing happen to the cage, white smoke appeared and an alarm started to blare. When the switch was hit again, two sprinklers extended from the top of the cage, and water sprayed everywhere.

Locked inside the cage, Ji Zhinan darted about everywhere,

trying to dodge the sprays, and his shouts of alarm were heard by the man on the line. He was even more anxious than Ye Qin, and he asked urgently, "What's wrong? What happened?"

Despite dodging in time, Ji Zhinan still ended up with half his body soaked. He was afraid of water, but he was also unwilling to seem a fool in front of the cameras. Swiping up his wet hair, he said dejectedly, "We failed...I want to go home."

This was a recording for a show, and Ye Qin thought that the man on the phone would say something tactful and comforting, asking Ji Zhinan to finish the recording first. Unexpectedly, with almost no hesitation, the man said gently, "Sure. I'll go pick you up, and we'll go home."

After an intermission, the reserve player Ning Lan stepped up.

This person was a lot more stubborn. A locked case that couldn't be opened, he would just punch and kick at it. Only after being given three red cards by the show did he then restrain himself slightly, and grinning, he went to stand next to Ye Qin, both of them working together to solve the Eight Trigram Formation on the wall.

As they worked on coming up with the solution, Ning Lan's patience ran out, and he nudged Ye Qin with his elbow. "I didn't go to school much. Senior, how about you first tell me how to read these words?" "

Trying to recall what he learned in school, Ye Qin stammered through some of the words before scratching his head, embarrassed. "There's no point in knowing how to read them anyway. I can't understand how to arrange them."

Ning Lan's brain churned, and he directed his attention to a loophole in the rules. Tilting his head up, he spoke to the camera installed in a corner of the room. "Calling for aid would get one of us eliminated. However, what if someone called us instead?"

As though there was an invisible bond between him and someone, not too long after his question, the phone in Ning Lan's pocket started ringing.

"Why are you taking so long?"

It was a young man's voice, and it even sounded a little familiar.

Ning Lan glanced at the time. "It's not twenty minutes yet, but we haven't even solved one room. Don't wait for me outside anymore, look for a place to rest first."

That person said plainly, "No."

"Why?" Ning Lan switched the phone to his other hand as he continued fiddling with the locked box with his right hand. "I think I'm going to need a lot more time here. It's so cold over there, go look for a place to have some coffee and snacks."

The man on the other end of the call still refused, saying stubbornly, "I only eat the food you make."

Ye Qin looked very sedate, but internally, he was speechless at how this couple was chatting and publicly displaying their affections in front of the cameras. Having a relationship between band members was really different, it seemed, looking at how they were so calm about it. In his mind, Ye Qin was furiously jotting down notes, deciding that next time, he would do this too.

After that, the two people coordinated their efforts, passing through the stages as they chatted away, only for them to be unable to pass the final stage no matter how they tried. When Ning Lan and Ye Qin showed off their special ability (shamelessly pleading and begging), the show finally gave them a chance, asking them to play charades, and promising they would receive an important hint if they won.

Ye Qin was aware that he wasn't familiar with Ning Lan, and they didn't share any tacit understanding of each other. As such, he wasn't sure if they would be able to make the guess within thirty seconds.

While he was all aflutter with nerves, Ning Lan burst out laughing when he saw the card. "You guys didn't do your homework properly. Senior and I will be able to solve this in seconds."

He then pointed at his own leg, then pointed at Ye Qin before winking slyly.

Just as he expected, Ye Qin was able to guess the answer. However, the answer was too embarrassing, and only after seeing that there wasn't much time left did Ye Qin say it aloud, blushing brightly.

Escaping successfully, Ye Qin looked at their timing of two hours, fifteen minutes and two seconds on the board mournfully. Ning Lan gave a stretch, consoling him, "Don't be disheartened. At least we escaped properly and without breaking any rules. I heard that there was a very famous idol who, after not being able to solve the last round, kicked the door down."

Ye Qin was speechless. "..." How someone mock their band leader and partner like that?

The recording concluded, and Ye Qin got into his car, words coming out unceasingly throughout the entire journey. He shared everything that happened during the recording with Cheng Feichi, even feeling disappointed that he hadn't been able to call him for help. "I shouldn't have performed so brilliantly, I should have feigned ignorance and given you a call."

Looking ahead of him, Cheng Feichi's lips curved into a smile. Ye Qin thought that he was laughing at him, and his eyes widened in a glare. "Are you thinking that I'm ignorant?"

Cheng Feichi shook his head. "No."

Ye Qin's cheeks puffed up. "Then what are you smiling at?"

His hands on the steering wheel, Cheng Feichi made a turn before saying placidly, "What else did you not tell me?"

Feeling guilty, Ye Qin looked everywhere but at him. "N-

no, there's nothing. I told you about everything that happened during the recording already."

Cheng Feichi lowered his gaze, glancing at Ye Qin's clenched fists that were resting on his thighs. However, he continued smiling, not saying anything.

Two days later, on the afternoon of February the 13th, in his office, Cheng Feichi received a text from Ye Qin.

[You really...want to see it?]

Contemplating for a moment, Cheng Feichi replied.

[Yes.]

Ye Qin didn't send any more texts in response.

When Cheng Feichi returned home that night, there was no one in the living room, only a cake lying on the dining table in solitude. There was no sign of the person who made the cake at all.

Cheng Feichi walked to the door of their bedroom, knocking on the door. Bangs and crashes could be heard inside, and then someone said, "Hold on for a moment, don't come in yet!"

Cheng Feichi waited by the door for ten minutes.

The door finally opened, but only half of Ye Qin's head poked out. His cheeks were burning red, and his lips were scarlet from being chewed on as well. Hemming and hawing, he said, "It doesn't...It doesn't look very good. Why don't we forget about it? Next time, we'll..."

Cheng Feichi pushed the door open. Wailing, Ye Qin spun around and fled back to bed, dragging the covers over him in an instant. Through the blanket, he said, his voice muffled, "Get out first...get out, please."

Cheng Feichi stood there, not moving an inch. "This is your birthday present for me?"

Hearing his voice, Ye Qin thought that he was angry. He hurriedly stuck his head out from under the covers, revealing long, wavy hair and a lace hairband. The pink blush on his

cheeks made him look even more radiant and exquisite, and he looked just like a shy little doll tucked under the blankets.

"Gege... Happy birthday."

Ye Qin finished speaking to see that Cheng Feichi's expression was still unreadable. As he took a deep breath, he closed his eyes, then in great determination, he flung the covers away, revealing a corner of a blue pleated skirt as well as the fair, gleaming thighs under the piece of clothing.

By the time his whole leg could be seen, Ye Qin was so embarrassed that he was about to cry. His voice trembling, he said meekly, "Here, it's what gege wanted to see...the s-sexy legs of a girl group member."

Standing by the bed, Cheng Feichi asked, "Who said I wanted to see that?"

Ye Qin first froze, then he heaved a large sigh of relief. He sat up, tossing his long hair behind him, a few curls hanging loosely over his collarbones that were exposed by his collar. "So you actually don't like them... Then I'll remove all this now. It's really too uncomfortable, being dressed like this..."

When he lifted his hand to take his hairband off, his cropped top lifted up as well. Ye Qin didn't realize that his supple waist was now revealed, and right after that, his wrist was caught.

Cheng Feichi's head bowed low, and in his deep, dark eyes lurked something that couldn't be read.

From his height, he looked down at Ye Qin who was kneeling on the bed. His voice husky, he said, "Who says I don't like it?"

Cheng Feichi later proved how much he liked it with his actions, pressing on with no breaks from the night of his birthday to the early hours of Valentine's Day.

In the morning, when Ye Qin woke up, all he could feel was the aching of his back and waist. It was even more exhausting than playing ten escape rooms. Upon seeing the long stockings

hanging by the edge of the bed when he opened his eyes, Ye Qin was dizzy, and recalling how that pair of stockings had been peeled off him last night, his face was hot enough to cook an egg.

After struggling for a few times, he still couldn't get up, and so he remained lying in bed, playing on his phone. The episode of the show Ye Qin had guest-starred in was about to be broadcast. Receiving a notification that he had been tagged by the official Weibo account of the show, Ye Qin first shared the post, then tapped into the pages of the two guests he worked with in the episode and scrolled through them.

Ji Zhinan didn't post anything today, and the last thing he did was liking a post by someone called "ReachForAStar." The location of that post came from Tromso, Norway, and the photo attached was of a flurry of snow, as well as brilliant northern lights streaking across the dark blue night sky. Nothing was said in the caption except for a moon and a star emoticon, looking like two people nestling up to each other.

As for Ning Lan, he had posted something, wishing everyone a happy Valentine's Day, and to have a good meal and drinks. Accompanying the post was a table full of dishes. A large plate of juicy, golden fried chicken in the center was especially eye-catching, and it made Ye Qin, whose stomach was currently empty, drool heavily.

The door was slightly ajar, and footsteps could be heard drawing closer. Ye Qin put his phone down, preemptively pulling his hands out from under the blankets before shutting his eyes and pretending to sleep. He planned on waiting for that person to walk to the bed and then jump on him with his arms wide open, seeking a Valentine's Day hug that belonged only to him. He was completely unaware that the curve of his lips had long exposed his dastardly plans.

EXTRA 12

Women's Day

TODAY, as the production crew was made up entirely of women, Ye Qin was able to finish work early. Sitting in the resting lounge, he was learning how to tie his shoelaces.

When Cheng Feichi arrived, even through the door, he could hear Ye Qin muttering away. As he pushed open the door, the person inside immediately fell silent. Unintentionally exposing what he was doing previously, Ye Qin raised his foot and kicked the air, complaining, "These shoelaces are so short and slippery, they can't be tied at all."

Cheng Feichi walked over, kneeling down and helping him tie them. As his hands moved, he repeated what he heard just now. "Bunny ears, bunny ears, playing by a tree..." Then, he lifted his head and asked, "What's the next line?"

Ye Qin was extremely embarrassed. Seeing that Cheng Feichi was quietly waiting for the next line, he took in a deep breath and said softly, "Crisscrossed the tree, trying to catch me... Bunny ears, bunny ears, jumped into the hole."

With every phrase he recited, Cheng Feichi would strictly follow his instructions.

When Ye Qin finally reached the last line of the rhyme,

"Popped out the other side beautiful and bold," Cheng Feichi tightened the bow knot, his eyes lowered, making the loops even. He then asked, "Our mother taught you that?"

Ye Qin was surprised by the form of address, and it took him a moment before he nodded. "Mn. Mom taught me when I was a child. At the time, I thought that this was a pain, and I didn't want to learn. So, every day, I would wait for her to tie my shoelaces for me. With no other choice, she found this nursery rhyme and taught it to me, but despite memorizing it, I still couldn't tie my laces."

The two chatted casually about Ye Qin's mother. Seeing how engaged Ye Qin was in the conversation, Cheng Feichi patiently asked, "What happened after that?"

Talking about the past, especially when it came to his mother, Ye Qin's heart was full of tenderness, and his smile was so wide that his eyes were curved into lines. "After that? From then on, she only bought me shoes without shoelaces. My mother and I, we're of one heart. We don't like things to be troublesome."

They were going to have dumplings for dinner that night, and Cheng Feichi was currently kneading the dough for the dumpling wrappers.

Standing next to him, Ye Qin studied his actions earnestly before stepping up to the plate. However, the wrappers he rolled out were either too thick or too thin, or else they were very oddly shaped and not circular at all.

As such, he gave up on rolling out any more wrappers, resting his chin in his palms and continued watching Cheng Feichi instead. Cheng Feichi worked the rolling pin with one hand as he turned the dough with his other. As he moved cleanly and deftly, pieces and pieces of dumpling wrappers appeared, round and perfectly flat, looking even nicer than the ones pressed out by a machine.

Ye Qin, who was learning how to cook, was full of both envy and admiration. Bursting with curiosity, he asked, "Who did you learn such skills from?"

Without a pause in his movements, Cheng Feichi answered placidly, "My mother."

During dinner, Ye Qin prepared two extra bowls of dumplings, along with a saucer of vinegar mixed with sesame oil.

Faced with a questioning look from Cheng Feichi, Ye Qin explained, "They're for our mothers. Both of them like lighter flavors, I'm sure they'll definitely enjoy a meal together."

After dinner, the two people headed downstairs for a walk to help digest what they ate. Cheng Feichi asked, "Since you're now addressing my mother as yours, then, how should you address me?"

Ye Qin answered with no hesitation, "Gege, of course."

"Think about it again."

Ye Qin keenly sensed that his boyfriend was laying a trap for him. His eyes darting everywhere, he said, "Lao...lao..."

"Lao-what?" Cheng Feichi continued guiding him.

Ye Qin had long been bothered by this issue, and after repeating "lao-" for some time, the smile on his face turned sly. He threw an arm over Cheng Feichi's shoulders, crisply calling out, "Hah! Lao-ge!"

He was then dragged home by his lao-ge to experience a sweaty and breathless lesson of love.

After undergoing this shower of love, Ye Qin was completely limp and exhausted, and he barely even had the energy to catch his breath. All he could think about was the embarrassing form of address Cheng Feichi used while asking him if he felt good during the bout of exercise.

Lying beside his pillow, his phone chimed. Struggling, Ye Qin reached an arm out to tap on his phone, opening the voice message Zhou Feng had sent him. "It's the second of February, the Longtaitou Festival! Bro, let's go get our hair cut together!"

At the same time, in another place, Zhou Feng waited and waited, but he did not receive a response. Only after sending another voice message to Ye Qin did he realize he had been blocked.

Question marks surrounded Zhou Feng's head. "What did I say wrong?"

"Perhaps Ye-tongxue is busy, and he's unable to go and cut his hair with you."

As he spoke, Liao Yifang picked up the electric hair clippers that had just arrived. He turned it on and the buzzing sound filled the room, its vibrations so loud that Zhou Feng's scalp tingled.

However, Liao Yifang was very satisfied by the power of the hair clippers. The way he looked at Zhou Feng's thick, dark hair was as though he was looking at a rich, juicy experimental subject. Pleased, he patted the chair next to him. "Come sit here, I'll help you cut your hair. In the future, we'll just cut our hair at home. It's convenient, we'll save money, and we won't be wasting any public resources as well. It's killing three birds with one stone."

The next morning, Ye Qin accepted Zhou Feng's friend request for the umpteenth time, and the two friends gave a like to the other's photos that had been newly posted the night before.

Zhou Feng had posted a selfie, and in the photo, his hair was even shorter than what was normal for a crew cut. It could be seen that both sides of his head had been shaved, and despite looking as though he was about to cry, he still deliberately added a breezy, cool caption: *"My new hairstyle, a guaranteed lady killer /proud"*.

As for Ye Qin, he had posted a photo of a plate of dumplings, wishing all his female friends a happy Women's Day. At the end,

there was a line that came out of nowhere: *"Hubby made them, they're extremely delicious <3"*.

After this business-like trade of mutual likes, the two of them commented under each other's posts simultaneously.

Zhou Feng: *[Simp /scorn]*

Ye Qin: *[Simp /eye roll]*

EXTRA   13

520

WAKING up that morning, Cheng Feichi's complexion was rather awful, and he looked quite listless.

Ye Qin asked him if he was feeling unwell, but he claimed he was fine. Worried, Ye Qin wanted him not to go to work, but he laughed as he asked, "Is it that you want me to stay at home and celebrate the occasion with you?"

Embarrassed, Ye Qin's eyes darted everywhere. "When did I say that? Anyway, 520 isn't an important occasion at all..."

To show how he didn't care about the day at all, Ye Qin personally walked Cheng Feichi to the door. Throughout the entire day, he didn't harass him with calls or text, obediently waiting for him to come home instead.

Cheng Feichi returned home very early in the afternoon. When Ye Qin saw that familiar car through the window, he leapt up from the couch, running to the door, opening it and welcoming Cheng Feichi home. Immediately, he realized something was wrong. "Why does your complexion look even worse?"

"Hmm?" Cheng Feichi seemed to not understand what he was saying, and he changed the topic instead. "The car is parked right outside. I'll change and we can leave."

Ye Qin grabbed him on the shoulder, turning him around and placing his other hand on his face. He felt an abnormal warmth exuding from him, and with wide eyes, he said in alarm, "Are you running a fever?!"

Ever since they met, Ye Qin had never seen Cheng Feichi with a fever before.

Or rather, to be a little more accurate, he had never seen him ill before.

Cheng Feichi had a very healthy constitution, so healthy that Ye Qin, a person that would have either a headache, stomach ache, or a cold every few days, extremely envious. He would always ask the other man if his body was forged with iron, and he had never heard him complain about any discomfort anywhere before.

Older generations often remind the young to not talk without thinking. This was especially so for things like "never losing money" or "never falling sick," and if they heard them saying so, a sound smack could be heard. Ye Qin was very remorseful now, and he kept feeling that Cheng Feichi would fall ill this time was all because of what he said. In the past, Cheng Feichi would be fine even after showering with cold water, but why did he have a fever now?

Cheng Feichi did not know to react to that. "It has nothing to do with you; I just accidentally caught a cold last night."

"But that has something to do with me as well." Ye Qin insisted on laying the blame on himself. "Last night, I was the one who opened the window a-and even removed all your clothes, while I was the only one under the blanket..."

Due to feeling ashamed, his voice grew smaller and smaller. In the end, his face was a bright red, and he looked more like that one having a fever than the one lying sick in bed.

"It's not entirely due to that," Cheng Feichi consoled him. "The main thing was that I had worked up quite a sweat, and the

wind was quite cold…"

Embarrassment overwhelmed Ye Qin so much that he could not lift his head. "Don't say any more, please."

Cheng Feichi thought for a while, then continued, "How about you give me a little of that blanket next time…"

The mortifying images from last night revolved around his head, and Ye Qin covered his face with his hands. "I'll give it, I'll give it! Next time, we'll both be under the blanket!"

The topic finally came to an end. Cheng Feichi set his alarm, and before he shut his eyes, he said, "I'll take an hour's nap, then I'll wake up and celebrate the occasion with you."

Ye Qin promised readily, saying that the time was perfect for him to look through his script.

Upon waking up, Cheng Feichi discovered that the sky outside was already dark. With some difficulty, he extracted his arm from Ye Qin's embrace. Groping about for his phone, he looked to see that he had actually slept for an entire three hours, the alarm he set having been switched off at some unknown time.

Ye Qin woke up as well, snuffling about and nuzzling further into Cheng Feichi's arms. He lifted his head forward, pressing the two foreheads together. "J-just sleep a while more. Like this, you'll recover faster."

Cheng Feichi did not understand. "Like this?"

Ye Qin again nudged forward, the tips of their noses pretty much touching each other. "Like this, half the excess heat in your body can be transferred to me."

This was the first time Cheng Feichi had heard about such a miraculous "medical treatment," and he couldn't help but laugh. "Are you sure this method works?"

Shutting his eyes, Ye Qin gave a little hum. "If it doesn't

work, then, gege can...can just hit me."

The 520 date that had been planned since a long time ago was now instead spent in bed. Cheng Feichi felt apologetic, and he wanted to take a rain check. However, Ye Qin said generously, "It's all right. I've already called to cancel our reservation. Only 20% of the booking fee was deducted, so we basically didn't spend any money at all."

Cheng Feichi was once again tickled pink by Ye Qin's unique style of consolation, and he complied. "Mn. With you around, we even saved the doctor's fees."

Completely forgetting how much work was done by the medication, Ye Qin patted his own chest in pride. "In the future, just look for me when you're sick." He thought for a moment, then added gravely, "Of course, it's best if you don't fall sick."

Cheng Feichi's fever was taken very seriously by Ye Qin. Waiting on Cheng Feichi dutifully, he watched him closely for quite a number of days. Only when he no longer felt any abnormal warmth whenever he pressed their foreheads together did he then relax.

Cheng Feichi asked him not to be overly anxious, but Ye Qin came up with all sorts of ridiculous reasons. "How could I do that? This is the first time you're experiencing a fever, and it's even because of me! I need to take full responsibility!"

Cheng Feichi froze.

This was actually not his first time.

One Chinese New Year a few years back, Cheng Feichi followed his mother to the south, arriving at S-City; which was a lot warmer than the capital. Out of nowhere, he started to feel weak in the limbs, and a fever came over him.

At first, he thought that it was due to the injury on his hand becoming infected. Later on, his temperature kept getting higher, and despite taking medication, the fever did not recede.

As he was applying for his visa, he nearly fainted at the counter. Only then did he realize that he couldn't just stubbornly push through this, and finally, he went to the hospital.

Over the next few consecutive nights, he dreamed.

The dreams were different, but the person was the same—Ye Qin was laughing, Ye Qin was crying, Ye Qin was falling asleep while working on his homework, Ye Qin was tugging at his hand while calling him gege.

The fever raged through Cheng Feichi, leaving him muddle-headed. A large portion of the time, he didn't even know if he was awake or asleep. He took this moment as the final time, the final time that he would allow himself to indulgently think about Ye Qin, to audaciously imagine every manner and characteristic of Ye Qin in his dreams.

He thought, since he had already said that they broke up, in the future, he wouldn't be able to see him laugh, to accompany him when he cried, to help him with homework, or to hear him call him gege again.

This was the final time.

What Cheng Feichi didn't know was, at that time, far away in the capital, Ye Qin was having a fever as well. In the younger boy's fantastical dreams, he was also giving in to his yearning that had nowhere else to go.

He dreamed that Cheng Feichi had gone to somewhere very, very far away. He was living there, studying there, and he made many friends there. Over there, he was living very happily.

Waking up, Ye Qin remained lying in bed, smiling, sincerely hoping that what he dreamed was real.

Smiling and smiling, he started to cry again, his chest heaving violently as steady streams of tears spilled from his eyes. Rolling down his checks, the tears seeped into his hair, soaking his pillow.

He refused to open his eyes, he refused to sit up, and stubbornly, he wanted to grab onto this dream. Lifting his hand, he desperately wiped his tears away. As he clenched his jaw tight, forbidding himself to cry, he forced the corners of his lips up, making himself continue smiling.

Cycling between bouts of crying and smiling, he was like a madman, delirious from his fever.

Ye Qin felt that, if all this could come true, he should feel happy for Cheng Feichi.

Even if he wouldn't be able to see him again anymore.

The preparation they made ahead of time for this year's 520 wasn't entirely wasted.

That night, Cheng Feichi found an origami star next to his pillow. He opened it to find words inscribed untidily within.

The morning after, Ye Qin too found an origami star next to his pillow. Hiding in the bathroom, he opened it up excitedly. Over and over again, he confirmed it, and he had no choice but to accept that Cheng Feichi had actually copied him word for word.

[Taking this day to wish that my other half would spend his every day in happiness, and all the best!]

Ye Qin was all puffed up in anger, but the anger also only lasted for a little while. When his finger touched those words written in a completely different handwriting that was bold and powerful, especially upon drawing across the words "other half," his lips curved upwards, and no matter how he tried, he couldn't hide his smile.

In the past, he never understood the meaning behind calling someone their "other half." Whatever he wanted, he must have it whole. What was the point of having only half of it?

Later on, he understood. Crying alone, smiling alone, romping about alone, having a fever alone...if one's heart was

empty, and if the other person wasn't present, then nothing was worth remembering.

You're a half, and I'm a half. Only together can we then become a complete heart that cannot be split apart, a love that cannot be torn apart.

EXTRA 14

Teacher's Day

YE Qin didn't have to go to work today, and early in the morning, he was woken up by someone knocking on the door. Rubbing his eyes blearily, he walked out of the bedroom to see Wei Jiaqi standing in the living room, holding a bouquet of fresh flowers and a fruit basket.

He greeted Ye Qin. "A good morning to Mr. Cheng's spouse."

Surprised, Ye Qin responded "Good morning" dazedly, then he heard Cheng Feichi ask, "Have you had breakfast yet?"

"I have. I still need to go to work later, so I won't be disturbing you any longer." Wei Jiaqi put the items in his hands down. "Mr. Cheng, again, my best wishes for this day."

Only after washing his face and brushing his teeth did Ye Qin finally realize what day it was today.

While eating breakfast, Ye Qin looked at the flowers displayed on the table, exclaiming, "It's already been so many years, and he still remembers that you were his teacher."

Recalling the days when he was cycling to his student's house to work as a tutor, Cheng Feichi chuckled. "I asked him to not treat me as his teacher anymore, but he refused to listen."

Ye Qin bit on his chopsticks, lost in thoughts. "A teacher

for a day, a..."

Cheng Feichi asked, "What?"

Ye Qin shook his head vigorously. "Nothing, nothing."

After breakfast, Cheng Feichi headed to his office. It was rare for Ye Qin to not have to go to work, and thus he went back to bed.

Lying down, he tossed and turned, unable to fall asleep. In the end, he gave Liao Yifang a call. "Happy Teacher's Day, Mr. Liao."

Liao Yifang was very touched. "Thank you, Ye-tongxue!"

Ye Qin flipped around, lying prone in bed. "Did you receive a lot of gifts today?"

"I did." There was a joy that couldn't be concealed in Liao Yifang's voice. "My students gave me cards as well as flowers, and I'm currently looking for a vase to put the flowers in."

Ye Qin asked, "That guy didn't give you anything?"

Liao Yifang was a little shy when Zhou Feng was mentioned. "He did. It's just been carried up to the office."

Ye Qin asked him what exactly he received that needed to be carried up, and Liao Yifang sent him a photo in response. Opening it up, Ye Qin saw a simple wooden plaque inscribed with bright golden words: *A great teacher has students everywhere.*

Ye Qin was speechless: "..." That was too stupid. It was definitely something he couldn't copy.

Cheng Feichi didn't come home at noontime. Ye Qin went out alone, before heading back home and taking another nap.

In the afternoon, he tidied up the house, paying not much attention to his tasks, then washed and prepared the ingredients they would be having for dinner. Picking up his phone, he saw that he hadn't received any calls or texts, but upon seeing what time it was, he started to get a little anxious.

Dialing Cheng Feichi's number, Ye Qin cleared his throat. "You're still busy?"

"Mn. I have a meeting later."

Ye Qin hemmed and hawed. "Then... Is your assistant around?"

"She's not, she's preparing the documents needed for the meeting." Cheng Feichi asked, "Is there a reason you're looking for her?"

Ye Qin was slightly panicked. "Is she in charge of your mail?"

"Mn. What did you send me?"

Starting to feel a little embarrassed, Ye Qin said, "N-nothing."

Cheng Feichi chuckled, and footsteps could be heard over the phone. "However, things like silk banners are sent directly to me."

Taking advantage of how he couldn't be seen in a phone conversation, Ye Qin feigned ignorance. "What...banner?"

"Perhaps it was sent by an ex-student of mine." Cheng Feichi stood still, and it sounded like he was rummaging for something. "The sender didn't put their name down. I don't know who it is."

Ye Qin started to get anxious again, and beating around the bush, he hinted, "I used to be...your student as well."

"Hmm?" It was as though Cheng Feichi had just come to the realization as well. "Oh? It's seems like that's the case."

By now, if he still couldn't hear that Cheng Feichi was deliberately teasing him, Ye Qin would truly be a fool.

Huffing and puffing, Ye Qin snorted loudly. Still, he didn't dare to defy his teacher, and he gentled his voice, saying cutely, "Then...can Mr. Cheng finish work earlier today?"

"You need something?"

Ye Qin bit his lip. "You've already accepted the silk banner. As a teacher, shouldn't you take responsibility for what you've done?"

Cheng Feichi held back his laughter. "What responsibility?"

"It's all written on the silk banner..."

Cheng Feichi thus recited, "An excellent teacher?"

"There's an accompanying phrase." Ye Qin's voice grew smaller. "The next part...is the key point."

That night, Mr. Cheng took responsibility with great earnestness, and Ye-tongxue was exhausted but happy.

The next day, Ye Qin wanted to laze in bed, gripping on tight to the covers and refusing to get up. The hoarseness in his voice was very obvious.

Cheng Feichi got out of bed first. On his way to the kitchen for warm water, he went past the living room and caught sight of how there had been a slight change in the silk banner on the table.

He drew closer, and the first thing that caught his eye was the two lines of words in gold right in the center of the red cloth: *An excellent teacher; full of love and consideration.*

The difference with the previous one was that the second line had been emphasized with a circle and a star.

Yesterday, Cheng Feichi had been amused by the banner, and looking at it right now, he was still tickled pink.

He recalled the little fellow from the past—how he would call out "Mr. Cheng"; how he would grab his arm and swing it as he whined about how he was unable to memorize the short English passage he was assigned; how he would try to use kisses to avoid the punishment of having to copy the passage out only to purse his lips aggrievedly when his attempt failed; and how he would secretly add his initials on the announcements of competition results... These were all memories he kept like treasures in his heart, and each time he recalled them, they would gleam even brighter.

His line of sight drifted downwards. Other than the two lines, there were two more lines of handwritten words added to the place printed with the date when the banner was gifted. It seemed like the writer hadn't been able to find a marker of the same color, or they had been extremely sleepy while writing, and so they didn't care about how it looked.

Written conspicuously was "Respectfully from 2nd Year Class 2, Ye Qin," accompanied by more words, smaller and messier.

He presumed that words written so covertly couldn't be something proper and polite. Cheng Feichi lifted the silk banner closer to his eyes, and he first froze before the corners of his lips curved up, a gentle amusement appearing in his eyes.

Late last night, Ye Qin, his waist aching and his limbs weak, secretly climbed out of bed, grabbing a random marker and going to the living room.

On the silk banner he had ordered in such a hurry that he didn't state his name, he wrote his name down as though marking his territory. Then, chewing on the marker cap, Ye Qin reflected for some time, and with a blush, he added a line in the corner: *A teacher for a day, a husband for life.*

At the end, he drew a cute, plump heart.

EXTRA 15

Mid-Autumn Festival

THE past few days, Ye Qin had been behaving a little strangely. Whenever he had nothing to do, he would be on his phone, staring blankly at the screen. Even if one was to call out to him a few times, he wouldn't react, and when he was asked if anything was wrong, he would shake his head and say everything was fine.

Cheng Feichi quietly asked his assistant, Xiao-Yun, to find out what was going on. It turned out that Ye Qin's boy band, that was still existing only in name, had created some anniversary merchandise to sell. There were badges, acrylic figures, dolls, and various other items. Each member of the boy band had their own set, and each set was sold separately.

Xiao-Yun said, "This sort of merchandise is released every year. Over the past few years, the sales of Mr. Ye's merch have been rather...rather dismal. You should have heard about such situations among fans before. How much they earned wasn't crucial, the important thing was their sales figures, and if it wasn't good, they would be mocked... But it's all right, as now, Mr. Ye doesn't rely on this for income."

With Xiao-Yun's guidance, Cheng Feichi browsed through

the Weibo Supertopic of Ye Qin's boy band, seeing many fans going all out to share and post about their idol's merch. There was quite a number of them declaring that they were going to buy a hundred sets to prove their worth as a fan.

However, there was only a few straggling fans who planned on buying Ye Qin's set. He had already changed his trajectory to being an actor, and it had been quite some time since he stepped away from being an idol. Adding the fact that he was already married, there were no longer as many fans that would brainlessly idolize him.

A small account had piped up in the Supertopic: *[Sisters, you don't have to work so hard. It's likely that there'll be YQ to take last place, so there's no worry about being embarrassed /giggle]*

A wrinkle appeared on Cheng Feichi's forehead, and his lips, pressed tightly together, turned down as well. So many years had passed, and Ye Qin's pride and desire to uphold his dignity were still innately carved deep into his bones. Although the competition for merch sales was both childish and pointless, Ye Qin was still secretly concerned about it.

He gave himself the target of hoping his sales at least wouldn't be an entire digit less than those of that brat, He Hansong. Before the release of the merchandise, he gave some of his friends a call.

"I'm not asking you to buy a lot... Since you've already said that, then I'll thank you first... Ah, sales start at 9:00 a.m. the day after tomorrow, don't forget..."

"Yuqing-jie, yes... The day after tomorrow. In the morning, you have... I have a gift for you, when I send the link over, you just have to tap to purchase. Any costs incurred, just expense them to me... No, no, no, it's not scalping...

"Yes, yes, yes, it's best if you buy more... Thank you, Yuqing-jie, I'll treat you to a meal next time!"

"Why are you acting all shocked? Can't your Qin-ge call

you? ...No, it's nothing, I just wanted to ask if you'll be busy the morning after tomorrow... No, I'm not buying you breakfast. Are you a pig? Always thinking about eating... How about this, you help me make some orders, and I'll let you drive my new car for two months?"

"Class monitor, are you busy? ...It's the day after tomorrow... Ah, you've already heard about it from Zhou Feng? ...Yes, it's a purchase, just like shopping online... You're worried that if you're too slow, it'll be sold out? You don't have to worry about that at all, your entire order will definitely be fulfilled, there's definitely enough stock in the warehouse."

Finding the matter embarrassing, Ye Qin didn't mention this to Cheng Feichi at all. Furthermore, this was nothing important. Cheng Feichi was normally busy enough with work, he shouldn't give him this extra worry.

Beyond all expectations, it turned out that Ye Qin had spent all his efforts for nothing. When the day of the sales arrived, the sets emblazoned with Ye Qin's name were all wiped out within ten seconds. One second, Ye Qin was still sending out links, reminding his friends to purchase them; the next second, after he refreshed the link, he was stunned to see the words "sold out."

His friends all said that they weren't able to buy any sets, and in the Supertopic, thousands of waves had been stirred up. Ye Qin's fans could now hold their heads up high, and one of them quickly created a gorgeous poster to heartily congratulate Ye Qin for having his merch sold out within ten seconds, tagging Ye Qin as well.

It had been years since something that brought him so much pride had happened. Ye Qin felt as though he was floating among the clouds. Giddy and delighted, he hurriedly liked the poster.

After liking, he didn't forget to copy that poster and share

it with Cheng Feichi, who was at work.

Ye Qin: *[/proud /proud /proud]*

This was a rare moment that Cheng Feichi played along with him.

Cheng Feichi: *[/Impressive /Impressive /Impressive]*

Ye Qin spent the next few days strutting about and bragging. During an event, he bumped into He Hansong, and this time, his aura was rather imposing. With his sales figures supporting him, Ye Qin did not cower, and his legs did not shake. His haughtiness from when he just debuted returned, and he angered He Hansong so much that the other man was seized with anger.

"Hah, trust you to inflate your own sales!"

Ye Qin's chest puffed up. "It's my popularity that made it that way! You can keep being jealous!"

Despite saying that, later on, when he calmed down, suspicion could not help but start welling up inside him. After the event, Ye Qin headed back to his company to try to find out more information, and he heard that all his merchandise had been bought by just one account. It was most likely some rich fan, and he then went to look for Xiao-Yun to have a chat. What he garnered from both sides corresponded with each other, and even a fool would know what had happened.

Ye Qin's emotions were rather complicated—forty percent embarrassment, mixed with thirty percent sweetness, twenty percent dilemma, and ten percent vexation.

The main thing he was in a dilemma over was their previous agreement to keep their work and personal lives separate. So what did it mean for Cheng Feichi to help his poor sales figures out?

Also, what was he going to do with all that extremely expensive merchandise?

The day before Mid-Autumn Festival was a workday. When

Cheng Feichi arrived at home in the evening, Ye Qin hurried about, bringing him tea and water. As Cheng Feichi headed to the bathroom for a shower, Ye Qin followed anxiously, stopping at the door. "Gege, do you want some mooncake?"

Cheng Feichi stopped unbuttoning his shirt, turning to look at the wide-eyed Ye Qin whose face was full of eager anticipation. A thought ran through his mind. Appearing like this, he did look rather similar to a mooncake.

He knew what Ye Qin wanted to ask, and he had no intentions of concealing it either. After his shower, and while they were eating mooncakes, he confessed to what he had done. "I'm the one who bought them. In the future, you don't have to worry about such things anymore."

"I wasn't worried at all." A warmth bloomed in Ye Qin's heart, but he still said stubbornly, "But now my fans can't buy any..."

Cheng Feichi laughed. "I'm your fan as well."

In the end, Ye Qin still got the rich fan to drag all the merch back home. Using his side account, he gave out some, and he didn't waste the rest, selling it online.

As he sold and sold, he then remembered something, and he asked Cheng Feichi, "If I didn't find out about it, how did you plan on dealing with all this?" "

"I'd have given them out as employee appreciation gifts."

Ye Qin's eyes widened. "That's not very appropriate, isn't it? Shouldn't you be giving out mooncakes or something during Mid-Autumn Festival?"

Cheng Feichi looked at him. "You're just like a mooncake."

"Uhh, uhh..." Stammering, Ye Qin was overwhelmed with shyness. "Uhh, if that's the case, I'm gege's mooncake, and no one else's."

Later, hearing that there truly were a lot of people in Cheng

Feichi's company who liked him and sincerely wanted his merch, while feeling proud, Ye Qin also felt that Cheng Feichi's reaction was too calm.

The evening of Mid-Autumn Festival, after dinner, Ye Qin asked tentatively, "With so many people liking me, won't you get jealous?" "

Cheng Feichi had brought some work home. His eyes shifted away from his computer monitor onto Ye Qin's face. "I won't."

Despite having an understanding of Cheng Feichi's personality, hearing this answer, Ye Qin was still a little dejected.

He rolled about on the bed, then looked out of the window, the bright moon reflected in his clear eyes. He suddenly settled down, and after some time, he propped his face up with his hands, asking Cheng Feichi, "At that time... Why did you choose me?"

Cheng Feichi looked up again, gazing at him, baffled.

"My temper's bad, I'm bad at studying, and I'm not devastatingly good looking." Ye Qin listed his flaws. "My motive for getting close to you...also wasn't that simple. There were so many people that liked you then, why did you choose me?"

Cheng Feichi stopped whatever he was doing.

He had never thought about this before.

He believed that liking someone was something that was very personal, and it was enough for him that it felt right. There was no need to seek other people's opinions, and there was even less of a need to examine the other person's strengths and flaws to decide if it was worthwhile.

Also, being human was to be flawed, thus needed to be understood and forgiven. He himself wasn't an exception.

Cheng Feichi put his work aside, walking over to the bed and gently placing his hand on Ye Qin's shoulder. Their bodies naturally drew closer.

"It's not just that," said Cheng Feichi.

"Huh?" Ye Qin was surprised.

"You're also prickly on the outside but softhearted inside, you insist on splitting hairs over insignificant things, and you trust others too easily."

Ye Qin was speechless. "..."

"However, in my eyes, all these points are adorable." Cheng Feichi met his eyes. "I like them all very much."

There seemed to be something magical about this "like." Ye Qin averted his eyes, his ears starting to burn.

Cheng Feichi pinched his earlobe. "You had too much to drink?"

Ye Qin pouted. "I didn't... Don't change the subject. Quick, answer me."

Cheng Feichi thought for a while, then answered, "There's no reason to it, I just like you."

Leaning over, Ye Qin slowly returned the hug. Although he didn't get a clear answer, satisfaction, more than regret, took over most of his heart.

Sprawled across Cheng Feichi's shoulder, he sighed softly. Closing his eyes, he said, "Thank...Thank you for still be willing to like me."

Later on, he still ended up distributing some of his merch to Cheng Feichi's employees as appreciation gifts for the Mid-Autumn Festival.

As everyone always greeted him respectfully as the boss's spouse, Ye Qin paid great attention to the sets he would be giving them. Not only did he tuck a few more autographed photos in them, he even personally wrapped them up. Just tying the bows alone, he spent half a day.

Watching him busy himself for an entire day, Cheng Feichi persuaded him to take a break. "Just leave them there, I'll

finish up."

Ye Qin then headed to the bedroom and lay down for a bit. When he came back out, he stared at the wrapped gifts on the table, examining them, a feeling that something was wrong running through him.

"You re-tied all the bows?" asked Ye Qin. "They're a lot prettier than the ones I tied."

"Mn," said Cheng Feichi.

Intuitively, Ye Qin smelled a rat. Before heading to Cheng Feichi's company, he secretly opened up one of the boxes. Alarmed, he discovered that the doll inside had disappeared!

On the way to the company to distribute the gifts, at Ye Qin's insistence, Cheng Feichi finally caved, sharing the reason why he took the dolls away.

The traffic light ahead shone red. Cheng Feichi took the doll from Ye Qin's hand, lying it prone on the car console.

Ye Qin asked, "... Its face is too ugly?"

Cheng Feichi shook his head, then pointed at the doll's butt.

Looking at where he was pointing, Ye Qin peeled the doll's pants off. His face burst into flames upon seeing the very perky, round butt.

Arriving at the company, Ye Qin finally came to a realization. Cheng Feichi did not want others to touch the doll's butt...

This was him being jealous, right?

Right?! Right?! This time, he really was jealous, right?!

Immediately, he was extremely excited, and he wanted to verify that instantly.

Ye Qin's fans were overly passionate. One by one, Ye Qin took a photo with them, and at the end, as everyone cheered and yelled, he jumped into Cheng Feichi's arms, finally finding a chance to ask him, winking, "Gege, are you jealous?"

Cheng Feichi had to laugh at the little guy's stubbornness. He tightened his hug, sidestepping the question as he whispered into Ye Qin's ear, "Thank you for choosing me as well."

The sun rises, and the sun sets. The moon waxes, and the moon wanes. Thank you for waiting, unafraid of loneliness, and thank you for still liking me, and being willing to be the solitary star in my long, chilly night.

Some follow-ups:

After the Mid-Autumn Festival, the story of the already-married sweet young thing Ye Qin and his partner was shared on the internet by some eyewitnesses, along with some embellishment. Many partners of stars and idols followed suit.

Ning Lan, the ex-band member and current partner of the superstar Sui Yi, woke up early that morning to buy his merch. He had his money all prepared already, but in the end, his fingers were still too slow. By the time he entered the link, there wasn't even a whiff of the limited-edition items left. He fell back into bed, frustrated. For quite a few hours, he didn't get up. Working outside, Sui Yi immediately posted on Weibo once he heard about it: *[Looking for one set of my merch that was released today, buying at high price.]*

Yi Hui, the fan and partner of the newly crowned Best Actor Zhou Jinheng, was a professional artist. Hiding behind an anonymous account, after providing the artwork for keychains and dolls for Zhou Jinheng's global fan club, he politely asked the club president if he could have a few dolls to hug to sleep at night. The president said that that wasn't a problem, but watching from the side, Zhou Jinheng expressed his unhappiness.

"The actual person is right here. Why do you want those stupid dolls? Just hug me."

As the fan club's vice-president, Mr. Qin Weiyu, the partner

of A-list actor Ji Zhinan, was more than prepared to deal with situations like this. With a few random clicks of his mouse, using his position, he vetoed the designs of doll clothes he deemed to be overly revealing with an easy conscience. As such, not too long later, Ji Zhinan held a doll dressed in a thick down jacket. His expression was rather complicated, and he started to say something, only to stop.

Ah, what a happy Mid-Autumn Festival!

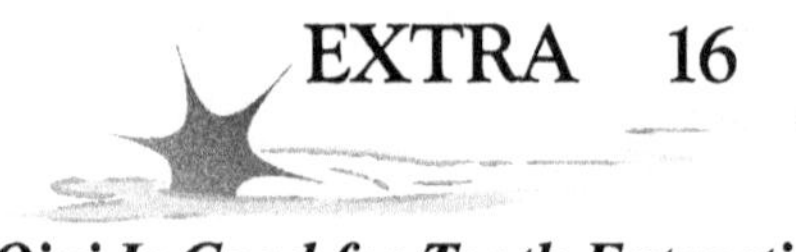

EXTRA   16

Qixi Is Good for Tooth Extraction

THE night before Qixi, Ye Qin was lying on the bed in the hotel booked by the production crew, video chatting with Cheng Feichi.

The chat was an instructional session, the sort that was very upright and proper.

Cheng Feichi's right hand had been injured before. The injury had been very deep, cutting into the tendons. As he did not manage to get any stitches and treatment in time, the injury had left his hand with chronic issues. He didn't have any problems with basic movements, but he wasn't able to exert too much strength with it.

Ye Qin felt that his involvement with this injury couldn't be denied, and thus he went everywhere to look for ways to heal Cheng Feichi's hand. Hearing that massaging could promote effective circulation of energy through the body, he would help Cheng Feichi massage his hand every night before bed.

Afraid that missing any massage session would cause the treatment to be affected, when he wasn't at home, he would insist that Cheng Feichi massage his hand himself.

"First, go along the lines of your palm... Then reverse... Use a little strength, you need to feel the heat coming off your skin,

or it'll be ineffective... Yes, just like this, then repeat a few more times... Does it feel warm yet?"

Cheng Feichi shook his head. "No."

"That shouldn't be the case..." Ye Qin couldn't understand. "Normally, even when I'm massaging it any old way, your skin heats up."

"Mn," said Cheng Feichi.

Ye Qin scratched his head in puzzlement, not wanting the "treatment" to face a setback. In the end, he made a painful decision. "I'll come back earlier."

True to what he said, the next morning, he did two additional scenes, and in the afternoon, he flew back home.

"The geges and jiejies in the production crew are extremely nice. They knew that I have a family, and so once filming wrapped up, they let me go home."

Cheng Feichi took half-day leave, and right now, he was helping Ye Qin unpack the luggage he brought home. After hearing what Ye Qin said, he paused. "The 'geges'?"

Ye Qin immediately took his words back. "No, no, no, it should be da-ge! I'm acting as the female lead's younger brother again, so I got used to using that..."

"Seems like you're getting along well with them."

"Uhh, it's not too bad?"

"Then, do they know why you came home today?"

Ye Qin twisted his body over to hold Cheng Feichi's right hand. Blinking his big eyes, he looked at Cheng Feichi devoutly, anticipation written all over his face.

The two men looked at each other for a long time. In the end, it was Cheng Feichi who couldn't hold on any longer, lifting his hand up and poking at Ye Qin's cheek. "Come, let's go to the hospital."

The gum around one of Ye Qin's wisdom teeth had been

inflamed for quite some time already, and whenever the weather turned colder, it would become so painful that he couldn't sleep. As such, this year, Cheng Feichi had checked his schedule a while ago, and helped him book a dental appointment for tooth extraction.

Two hours later, Ye Qin was carrying his wisdom tooth as he left the treatment room mournfully.

Cheng Feichi was waiting by the door. "Was the dentist fierce?"

Ye Qin shook his head.

"Did he instruct you to eat less candy?"

Ye Qin shook his head again, and he lisped, "It wath my withdom tooth, not a rotted tooth."

Gently pressing an ice pack on Ye Qin's left cheek, Cheng Feichi then asked, "Does it hurt?"

Ye Qin shook his head sluggishly, only to start nodding halfway instead. "It'th not that painful, I jutht can't have a yummy featht anymore."

Today was Qixi, and crowds thronged the streets.

When they met with the third traffic jam of the day in the city, Ye Qin sighed. "Forget it. There'th tho many people, there mutht be no tableth left in the rethtaurant."

His hands on the steering wheel, Cheng Feichi looked at the long lines of vehicles in front of him. "We'll go home to eat then."

"The atmothphere, I wanted the atmothphere..." Ye Qin hissed in pain.

At this time, the effect of the anesthesia had worn off. Ye Qin cupped his face in pain, tears rolling about in his eyes.

Cheng Feichi turned to look at his swollen cheek. "If it's painful, then don't talk so much."

Ye Qin had always listened to what Cheng Feichi said, and so he shut his mouth obediently.

But unable to reconcile himself to remain quiet like this, Ye

Qin's brain churned on. Taking advantage of how they were still stuck in the jam, he leaned towards the driver seat, smacking a kiss on Cheng Feichi's face.

Perhaps it had been too long since he was kissed in public, Cheng Feichi was stunned for quite a few seconds.

Having successfully performed his sneak attack, Ye Qin's face was full of glee. "Gege, Happy Qithi!"

To do something like this, sooner or later, one would have to pay the debt.

When they arrived home, once the door closed behind them, Ye Qin was pressed against the wall, and Cheng Feichi returned the attack.

It was a French kiss, the sort that went very deep.

Only after the kiss ended did Ye Qin then remember he'd just had his tooth extracted. Still catching his breath, he covered his mouth, speaking in alarm, "All the medication went into your mouth!"

Cheng Feichi chuckled. "It's fine, it's sweet."

They were probably unwilling to spoil the atmosphere, and so the two people remained in the dim hallway for a while more.

Despite his toothache, Ye Qin was still filled with will. Taking that moment, he asked, "When I wathn't home over the patht month, did you mith me?"

Almost as though he didn't even need to think about it, Cheng Feichi answered, "I did."

Ever since they got back together, the two of them rarely said anything mushy in front of the other. Ye Qin's face burned upon hearing the response, and he snorted, "I don't believe you."

After some rustling, Cheng Feichi groped his way to Ye Qin's hands that were hanging by his sides, grabbing them. "If you don't believe me, touch this. Isn't it hot?"

A day of not seeing each other was like having spent three

autumns apart, and the fire of their passion blazed up to the skies.

Finished with their nighttime exercise, the two of them cuddled in their bed. One pressed an ice pack to the other's cheek, and one massaged the other's hand.

As he massaged, Ye Qin started laughing foolishly. "It'th warming up, it'th warming up. It really warmed up."

When they turned off the lights, about to fall asleep, Ye Qin was still worried. He turned to ask the person next to him, "When other people mathage your hand, doeth it warm up too?"

"You're the only one who has ever massaged it," said Cheng Feichi.

This time, Ye Qin was satisfied. Yawning, he shut his eyes, and groggily, he continued mumbling, "Why doeth it warm up..."

Ye Qin believed that he always had to live up to his idol image, and he felt that right now, he was extremely ugly. He wrapped a scarf around his face, refusing to remove it even when asleep, and he even insisted that Cheng Feichi lay on his back, not allowing him to turn to look at him.

Only when he heard Ye Qin's breathing even out did Cheng Feichi turn around, looking at the person next to him.

During that summer vacation in their second year of high school, just like tonight, he had gazed countless times at Ye Qin's side profile in the dark. Perhaps to fill up the emptiness of those five years, now, whenever he had the chance, he would quietly look at him for a long, long time, and he would never get tired of it.

In the tranquility, the ticking clock sped up the time that they had missed out on. His hand, now healed from its previous injury, lifted up, his warm fingers gently drawing across the face that was glowing slightly from the reflected light.

In the dark, Cheng Feichi opened his mouth, answering quietly, "Because it's you."

EXTRA 17

Halloween

THE night before Halloween, Ye Qin re-emphasized for the eighth time, "It's Halloween tomorrow."

Cheng Feichi: "Mn."

Ye Qin opened his arms wide, drawing a circle with them. "I can eat this much candy."

"That's too much."

Ye Qin pulled his arms in a little, drawing a small circle this time. "How about this much?"

"Mn."

Ye Qin said, "I've already prepared my basket to collect candy."

Cheng Feichi was confused.

Ye Qin: "It's that parcel I received today, that basket with a butterfly knot on it."

Cheng Feichi was speechless.: "..."

Ye Qin asked, "Is it a little too big?"

"No."

Ye Qin said, "Right, right? You don't think it's too big either."

"It's a lot too big."

"..." Ye Qin gave a very long sigh. "However, if it doesn't get filled, it means I'm not a fortunate young boy."

On Halloween, Ye Qin, his face painted for the day, searched the bed, the dining table, the coffee table, and the refrigerator. He found some candies, but they couldn't even cover the bottom of the basket.

A little unhappy, Ye Qin hugged his basket, declaring that he was going to go out and look for candy.

When he reached the door, he was called to a stop.

Holding no hope at all, Ye Qin pursed his lips, asking, "Trick or treat?"

Cheng Feichi did not say anything, only facing him and opening his arms wide.

A few minutes later, Ye Qin dug out a dozen or so more pieces of candy from Cheng Feichi's clothes, and his basket no longer looked so empty.

However, it was still far from being full. Ye Qin insistently believed that there was still candy hidden somewhere, and he rolled up his sleeves, starting to take Cheng Feichi's clothes off.

Cheng Feichi stated, "There really is none left."

Ye Qin replied, "I don't believe you!"

The candy hunt continued in bed.

Later on, unwrapping the last candy taken from Cheng Feichi's palm, Ye Qin shoved it into his mouth in satisfaction, sighing, "How sweet."

Occasionally, Cheng Feichi would believe the untrustworthy stories created by Ye Qin, and thus he decided to take the risk of tooth decay, heading out to buy more candy to fill up Ye Qin's basket.

Just as he sat up, pulling his clothes on, Ye Qin hugged him from behind.

"You don't have to buy any more candy, it's already full." He

nuzzled into Cheng Feichi's broad back, his eyes half-lidded in pleasure. "I'm really, really fortunate right now."

I'm Ye Qin, the most fortunate young boy in the whole wide world~

EXTRA 18

Ye Qin's Birthday #1

THE Chinese zodiac of this year was Ye Qin's animal. The day before his birthday, he received a package containing a dozen pieces of red underwear.

Everyone knew that Ye Qin was very particular about his appearance. Each time he stepped out of the house, from head to toe, from inside to out, he must be at the forefront of fashion trends, and thus this extremely tacky red underwear was clearly not purchased by himself.

He asked around, but it wasn't Yi Hui, Liao Yifang, or even that old geezer Ye Jinxiang. After pondering over it for some time, Ye Qin decided that it could only be Cheng Feichi.

That night, Ye Qin locked himself in the bathroom. Holding up a pair of red underwear in front of the mirror, he examined it, and a blush bloomed upon his face.

Honestly! If he bought them, he bought them. He could have just openly placed the package on the table at home! Secretly mailing them home was even more embarrassing, thought Ye Qin.

After showering, Ye Qin pulled on his new underwear and scrambled into bed. He dragged the blanket up to the tip of his nose and stared at the door in anticipation, looking just like a

186

new bride on her wedding night, waiting for her husband to come back into the room.

However, Cheng Feichi had to deal with work matters that night. He worked in his study until past ten, and by the time he showered and headed into the bedroom, Ye Qin was already asleep.

He walked over to the bed, tucking the man sprawled across it neatly under the blanket. With a glance, he noticed a flash of red around the younger man's waist.

A flick of his wrist, and the blanket parted a little. Upon seeing that pair of buttocks wrapped solidly by an old-fashioned pair of boxers, Cheng Feichi froze for a moment, before his brows knitted slightly.

It was the weekend the next day. Following their original plans, the two of them went to the aquarium, then to the restaurant they made reservations at.

In the middle of their meal, the server brought over a cake about six inches wide. Once Ye Qin saw it, he understood what was happening. Happily, he devoured a big half of the cake, praising generously, "It's even more delicious than last year's cake!"

Where they sat was an oasis of peace amidst the bustle. After their meal, they headed outside, and Ye Qin rubbed at his bulging belly as he puffed out balls of white. Obediently, he stood there, allowing Cheng Feichi to wrap a scarf thickly around him.

The two men took a short stroll down the quiet path, lit by the streetlights. Ye Qin held a hand out, and Cheng Feichi readily took it, tucking it into the pocket of his coat.

His eyes half-lidded, Ye Qin gave a sigh of satisfaction. When he stretched out his other hand, hinting that something was missing, a heavy weight, warm from body heat, landed in his palm.

It was a car key.

This year's birthday presents, other than a cake made by Cheng Feichi himself, for the first time in his life, Ye Qin received a car that truly belonged only to him.

Having not driven in many years, Ye Qin sat in the driver's seat, feeling an inexplicable anxiety. He trembled as he stepped on the accelerator, and when he made a turn, he leaned all the way out, looking at the traffic light. The two streets he drove through, his speed never exceeded thirty kilometers an hour, and he looked just like a newbie who had just received his license.

"In the past, when driving a manual transmission, we needed to step on the clutch with our left foot." Whenever he was nervous, Ye Qin would start rambling. He said, "This car is a lot better than the one I drove back then. I'm not very used to it."

In the passenger seat, Cheng Feichi had a hand on the steering wheel to help Ye Qin. "It's all right, just drive as you will."

With this sentence bolstering him, Ye Qin's courage swelled. As he drove a few kilometers on the suburban roads with few people around, he gradually regained his competence from years back.

"Back then, despite being on a bicycle, you were even faster than me in a car." Thinking about the past, Ye Qin could not help but grumble. "To shake me off, you even deliberately cycled down a path that cars couldn't go, and you were why I was caught by the police."

Looking at it now, it was rather incredible. Only Cheng Feichi himself knew how many tricks he had quietly employed to avoid Ye Qin's hot pursuit.

Ye Qin was still twisting himself into knots over the matters of the past. "Then, when it was raining so heavily, why did you refuse to get into my car?"

Thinking about Ye Qin's lack of doubt and his unconditional

trust ever since they met, Cheng Feichi let go of his grip on the steering wheel. "Now, am I not in your car?"

The experienced driver Ye Qin drove Cheng Feichi in his new car, happily heading home.

Back home, he shared a photo of his new car with his friends. Zhou Feng could not help exclaiming over it, asking Ye Qin if he could let him drive it for a bit.

Without a moment of hesitation, Ye Qin refused him with a very reasonable explanation. "Neither a car nor a wife can be lent out."

He then turned to sneak a peek at Cheng Feichi, only to see the other party lift his gaze from his computer screen over to him. Ye Qin hunched over a little, softly changing his words. "Neither a car nor a...husband can be lent out."

When he found a lollipop in his pocket, Ye Qin smacked his own forehead, scolding himself for being stupid. He had been asking Cheng Feichi the entire day, but he never thought that it would be hidden on himself.

Shoving the lollipop between his lips, Ye Qin suddenly came to a realization that he had overdone it on his sugar intake that day. Whenever he put on weight, it would become very evident on his face. He had a photo shoot next week, and if Yue-jie were to discover that he had put on weight, she was going to nag him again.

As such, Ye Qin did his first workout as a twenty-four-year-old—running back and forth along the longest path possible at home.

After ten or so laps, he asked Cheng Feichi, "Have I lost weight?"

This was very difficult to judge visually, and thus Cheng Feichi only said, "You're not fat."

Not assured by that, Ye Qin looked all over for a bathroom scale. Not finding it under the couch, when he stood up and turned his head, a pair of arms circled his waist out of the blue, and he was lifted straight up.

Ye Qin exclaimed in fright, his eyes rounding instantly.

Weighing him, Cheng Feichi was as relaxed as usual, With a very convincing tone, he said, "You've lost weight."

After a satisfying birthday, Ye Qin was very pleased.

It was just that when they were doing *that*, he experienced a bout of embarrassment over his bright red underwear, and the atmosphere was a little spoiled.

However, later on, when his ass cheeks turned red as well, they were rather complementary.

After the deed, Ye Qin complained. "And you even said I lost weight. Buying such loose underwear, were you afraid that I couldn't fit into them?"

Silence reigned for some time, and Cheng Feichi came in with the truth. "I'm not the one who bought them."

The tranquil night turned transformed into something tumultuous.

Ye Qin freed a certain best actor from the blocklist where he resided most of the time. Upon asking him if he was the one who sent the underwear, Ye Qin received a confirmation.

Zhou Jinheng replied, "Yup. The material's warm but breathable, so I got them straight from the factory. Are you happy with them?"

Ye Qin sent him a smiling emoji in return and sent him into the blocklist again.

The case was now solved, but the embarrassment remained. The strange atmosphere that couldn't be put into words lingered on to the next day.

During breakfast, Ye Qin tried his best to maintain his

dignity. "I heard that wearing red underwear during one's zodiac year helps you avoid disasters, so I didn't think too much about it and..."

"Mn." Cheng Feichi wasn't much bothered by the issue. "That's a good reason. They should be worn."

Ye Qin heaved a sigh of relief.

Then, that very night, Ye Qin received a dozen pairs of new red underwear.

"I heard that if they're given by someone close, the effect will be even better," said Cheng Feichi. "Just take them as your birthday gift."

By the time Ye Qin changed into the perfectly fitting new underwear in delight, he then recalled that he had already received quite a number of presents yesterday.

He couldn't help but marvel. "Ahh...it's so difficult."

"What's difficult?"

"It's so difficult not to feel that I've already won in life."

To prove it, Ye Qin pointed at his red underwear. "Mine."

Then he pointed at the already digested cake and lollipop in his tummy. "Mine."

Then he pulled out the car key from his pocket. "Mine."

Finally, looking as though to be very distraught, he concluded, "There are too many..."

Loosening his tie, Cheng Feichi looked over at Ye Qin. "There's more."

Ye Qin was confused. "There's more...?"

Cheng Feichi said matter-of-factly, "There's me as well."

Overwhelmed with bliss, Ye Qin rushed forward, dragging Cheng Feichi down by his collar and forcing him to lower his head. Standing on his toes, Ye Qin pressed a kiss on him.

Then, he was lifted up by Cheng Feichi, who then held him

against a wall and flooded him with kisses.

Still panting when their kisses concluded, Ye Qin eagerly clasped his hands around Cheng Feichi's neck, burying his face into the crook of the older man's neck and nuzzling into it. In a low voice, he declared, "Mine."

With their most treasured person in their arms, so close that they were one, both felt at ease. The indiscernible gap between them were filled up by their mingled breaths. Laying a gentle kiss on the soft rim of Ye Qin's ear, Cheng Feichi closed his eyes. He seemed to be echoing Ye Qin, but also seemed to be mumbling to himself.

"Mn, mine."

EXTRA   19

Cheng Feichi's Birthday #1

A year ago, the couple had taken a trip to the apartment where Cheng Feichi used to live.

Within that old, small residential area resided many people, and it was lively and bustling. Colorful lights and red lanterns were strung from the main entrance to the doorways of the apartment buildings, and every few steps would have a neighbor waving and greeting them.

As they headed upstairs, the resident of an apartment downstairs just happened to step outside. Upon seeing Cheng Feichi, the elderly man smiled as brightly as before. "Xiao-Cheng's back."

Following behind Cheng Feichi, Ye Qin greeted the old man with a "Mr. Li." After a quizzical gaze from the old man, he guiltily shrunk back behind Cheng Feichi.

"This little fellow looks quite familiar," murmured Mr. Li. "When Xiao-Cheng was in high school, you dropped by before, right?"

Thinking that the old man was referring to that time when he misunderstood and came here to investigate Cheng Feichi, Ye Qin buried his head even deeper into his chest. "Uhh... Yeah.

193

Yes, probably."

"At that time, Xiao-Cheng was no longer living here already."

Ye Qin did not expect that the conversation would take such a turn, that Mr. Li would be referring to *this* instead.

The old man said, "You were so young and stubborn, and despite meeting with failure a few times, you still refused to give up, knocking on every door and asking where the Cheng family had moved to…"

The more Ye Qin listened, the more embarrassed he became. However, it would be very impolite to stop the old man from talking about it, and instead, he tried dragging Cheng Feichi upstairs.

He didn't even manage to take two steps before Mr. Li spoke, the old man's words coming faster than Ye Qin could move. "I still remember that one time, it was also around the end of the year. You were sitting in the stairwell, wiping at your tears. I had thought that you were homeless, and so I asked my wife to cook a bowl of noodles for you. As you chanted happy birthday, you continued wiping away your tears, and you completely emptied the bowl."

When they headed upstairs, opening the door of the apartment and going in, Ye Qin remained silent for a very long time. He didn't look up at all, his eyes glued to the floor.

He didn't say anything, and thus Cheng Feichi didn't ask. Walking into the kitchen, Cheng Feichi first turned the main switch on, then he washed the kettle and boiled some water.

Their reason for coming here today was to do some spring cleaning. The apartment wasn't very big, but it was enough for the two of them.

Ye Qin went to the balcony to retrieve the broom, and he started from the little bedroom Cheng Feichi once lived in.

As he swept his way to the door, he heard Cheng Feichi on the phone discussing work matters.

During the last few months of the year, every industry and profession were busy. These few hours of free time together were something the two people had to work quite hard to coordinate.

As such, Ye Qin treasured this time even more. He hurriedly cleaned the floor, then washed a rag and started wiping.

Cheng Feichi's bedroom had long been emptied, and even the trophies in the cabinets had already been gathered up by Ye Qin and moved to their little home. As such, tidying up was rather easy. As for the other bedroom, it was where Cheng Xin used to live. There were still some books and magazines there, and afraid of causing any offense, Ye Qin planned on just doing some simple cleaning up and leaving right after that.

His intention was to just muddle through his work, but when he started cleaning up, he couldn't stop himself from becoming very particular. When he got to the desk, the dust arising from the narrow crevices between the drawers kicked off Ye Qin's obsession for cleanliness. Bending down, he rubbed for some time but still did not manage to get rid of the dust, and he could only pull the drawers out, planning on wiping the insides properly.

Perhaps due to being in disrepair, it was very difficult to pull the drawers out, and Ye Qin had no choice but to exert more strength into it.

He yanked a little too hard, and the drawer flew out. Ye Qin heard a smack on the ground, and he looked down to see a white envelope that had been stuck in the drawer's crevice. An exposed corner of the photograph within had yellowed with age.

The company had a lot of work to deal with at the end of the year. Cheng Feichi finished delegating the work during his phone conversation, and when he ended the call, the water was

already boiling.

He washed two glasses. Filling them up with water, he walked further into the apartment. Cheng Feichi discovered that everywhere he could see was gleaming and clean, including the floor.

He thought about how the same thing had happened last year during this time as well. Once they went in, he had to conduct a remote meeting over the phone, and by the time it was over, Ye Qin had already finished cleaning up. At that time, the younger man was curled up on the couch, deeply asleep. Upon being woken up, he had a look of unhappiness on his face, but when he started grumbling, it wasn't about how tired he was from doing the spring cleaning alone.

Instead, he complained, "Why did you take so long? I was about to be bored to death."

With this in mind, Cheng Feichi's footsteps quickened, thinking that he would still be able to catch up with Ye Qin and they could do the cleaning together.

However, when he opened the bedroom door, Ye Qin was standing by the desk with neither a broom nor a rag in his hands. Hearing someone enter, a fierce jolt ran through the smaller man, and he quickly hid what he was holding behind his back.

Feigning nonchalance, Ye Qin asked, "You're done? Quick, quick, quick, come and help."

Unfortunately, he wasn't especially skilled at covering up, and the envelope containing the photograph was lying out in the open, right in the middle of the desk. With one glance, Cheng Feichi knew what he was trying to hide.

If not for Ye Qin accidentally coming across this, Cheng Feichi had completely forgotten that in this apartment, there were still such photos; such things that seemed rather extravagant and wasteful to him in the past.

Seeing that he could not hide it, Ye Qin immediately surrendered. He held his hand out, but refused to let go. "Just let me keep one, all right?"

Cheng Feichi looked down at it. The youth in the photo had his lips tightly pressed together, and his eyes, looking at the camera, were full of apathy.

He remembered that this ID photo was taken for his Olympiad exam application. During that time, Cheng Xin was unwell, and he had to make frequent trips home and to the hospital. To take care of his mother, the young Cheng Feichi had nearly relinquished his chances of participating in the examination.

Those gloomy days seemed to have just happened recently, but also a long time ago. His eyes drifting away, Cheng Feichi saw how careful the fingers grasping the photo were, and he asked, "Why do you want to keep it?"

"Look at how handsome you were." Ye Qin lifted his chin in pride. "Gege's handsomeness has persisted since you were young. As a member of your family, I don't have to mention what a boost to the ego it is!"

His words made Cheng Feichi smile. Just as the corners of his lips quirked up, his eyes were covered by Ye Qin, who had ran behind him.

Despite already being used to how Ye Qin would do whatever popped into his head, Cheng Feichi was still surprised by this sudden action. In his abruptly darkened world, he frowned slightly and asked, "What happened?"

This was clearly also a sudden impulse from Ye Qin, moving before thinking. Now, he didn't know how to extricate himself from this situation, and he could only gulp and swallow his nervousness, before speaking, soft and slow, "It's in the past, it's all in the past. From now on, gege should just smile like this...and continue walking forward."

Due to their height difference, Ye Qin was on tiptoes. His chin, hooked over Cheng Feichi's shoulder, nuzzled affectionately into him, and he continued, "Leave all your unhappiness behind you, and don't ever look back again."

To fulfill his promise, in the days that came after, every time the two people left their home, Ye Qin would follow behind Cheng Feichi. He stayed neither too close nor too far, the distance about two to three meters apart.

This made Cheng Feichi want to laugh, but he also felt rather helpless about it. Ye Qin was very obstinate, and no matter how he persuaded the younger man, he refused to listen, swearing to be his "guardian" forever. The first night of the new year, after dinner, the couple had originally planned on watching a movie. However, all showings were fully booked, and they had to go for the next best thing, which was strolling along the streets.

Keeping his promise, Ye Qin was walking behind Cheng Feichi, asking him about what his arrangements for tomorrow were.

"It's the second day of Chinese New Year. Don't tell me that you'll still need to work?"

"I'll need to make a trip to the office in the afternoon."

"Ah, does your company give out birthday red packets?"

"Mn."

"Are you considered an employee?"

"I am."

"All right, then..." Since there was money involved, Ye Qin compromised. Dully, he said, "Why reject free money?"

Cheng Feichi turned towards him. "You had other plans for tomorrow?"

Ye Qin pursed his lips. "I did, but I've changed them now. I'll be waiting for you at home."

"You don't have to wait. Come with me to the office."

"Why would I go there?"

"To collect red packets."

"...It's not my birthday."

"But," said Cheng Feichi, "I don't want to let you wait any-more."

Ye Qin froze.

Five years was enough for a person to learn to wait. A thousand days and nights and more was a very, very long period, so long that Ye Qin almost forgot what he was feeling that year, when he sat under Cheng Feichi's apartment and wished that far away person a happy birthday.

He learned how to breezily hide away the pain and difficulties he experienced in the past. He learned to smile and let things go, just like how Cheng Feichi always easily forgot his wickedness and remembered his goodness, how he weaved his tenderness into a net, wrapping him intimately within it.

A short distance of two or three meters, yet it seemed as long as the compilation of those five years. However, this time, Ye Qin was no longer afraid, as no matter how far he fell behind, there would forever be someone who would look back at him.

The man, standing under a streetlight, was enveloped by the warm light cascading down onto him, his eyes, his gaze, including the hand he held out towards him.

The sounds of hurried footsteps were heard. Very quickly, a smaller hand was placed in the bigger one. Ye Qin had finally given up on his role as a "guardian", and now he stood beside Cheng Feichi.

The soft, supple net throbbed in pain from childish arrogance, and the thorns of the people inside the net had been silently ground away. They looked to be covered in wounds, but even if

history were to repeat itself, neither of them could bear to take a step back.

Fortunately, like a phoenix rising from the ashes, things would always grow, and wounds would always heal.

Ye Qin exhaled, looking forward. "Then, let's hurry up and go."

In that non-chilly night, side by side, the two people strolled leisurely amidst the glittering neon lights of the early spring.

"Oh right, how much will be in the red packet tomorrow?"

"How much would you like?"

"The more the better, of course... Ehh? Hold on. Your staff isn't expecting me to treat them to a meal, right?"

"Hmm?"

"It's Chinese New Year. I can be considered the boss's spouse."

"Then you should be treating them."

"Gege...."

"Hmm?"

"From now on, every step forward is a brand new one. I won't be standing still and waiting like a fool anymore... As for you, don't keep looking back anymore."

Faced with how Ye Qin had unscrupulously changed his tune, Cheng Feichi's response was to curl his fingers in further, holding Ye Qin's hand even more tightly.

Their fingers interlaced, their palms pressed against each other, their hearts beating and pulsing as one.

Ye Qin heard Cheng Feichi say, "Yes, we'll do that together."

We'll walk forward together, neither of us waiting, and neither of us looking back.

EXTRA 20

Cheng Feichi's Birthday #2

UNFORTUNATELY, Cheng Feichi's birthday fell on a Monday this year.

Ye Qin started planning their itinerary a month in advance, only to learn when the day approached that Cheng Feichi could only spare half a day. He shrugged, looking regretful and resigned. "Well, we'll just have to stick with somewhere close."

"Somewhere close" meant Disneyland in S-City.

A day before, he learned from Yi Hui that the park would be crowded. But since they were going at noon, it made little difference whether they went earlier or later.

Ye Qin went to the company to pick Cheng Feichi up. After getting off at their destination, he pinned a birthday badge on Cheng Feichi.

Cheng Feichi wore a lead-gray coat today, and the badge stood out rather conspicuously on his chest.

He looked down at it and pursed his lips, looking like he wanted to object.

Anticipating this, Ye Qin held the badge firmly in place so that he couldn't take it off. "You're not the CEO, Mr. Cheng, today," Ye Qin said seriously. "You're the happiest birthday boy

in this fairy tale world today."

Cheng Fei chuckled and let him have his way.

After entering, they were greeted by enthusiastic performers along the way. For each birthday greeting received, Ye Qin would also repeat "Happy Birthday" to Cheng Feichi.

Ye Qin had brought along a Polaroid camera. Occasionally, he would run ahead and assume a standard photographer's pose with his camera raised. "Look here! Look at the camera and smile... Perfect!"

It wasn't their first visit here, so they were in no rush to try all the rides. They sat on a roadside bench when they were tired and bought some street snacks when they were hungry. Even waiting in line didn't feel boring when they were together.

After watching the parade in the afternoon—when it was the most crowded—Ye Qin pulled Cheng Feichi into a gift shop. Picking up a hairband with furry ears, he stood on tiptoe to put it on for Cheng Feichi and quickly snapped a photo before the latter could react.

On their way back at sunset, Ye Qin awkwardly asked Cheng Feichi if he would go to one more place with him.

They got off at their destination in the suburbs to the greeting of the cool evening breeze against their faces. A field spread out before them, with a corner sectioned off, filled with sunflowers that had yet to bloom, leaving only sepal-covered buds drooping at the top of the fuzzy green stems. Ye Qin scratched his head in embarrassment. "I planted them too late, and the cold weather didn't help. They probably won't bloom until next month."

Cheng Feichi walked closer and looked down at the sunflowers. "You planted them?"

"Yeah." Ye Qin puffed out his chest, looking rather proud of himself. "I thought it'd be hard, but it was quite okay... Let's come back again when the weather's warmer, all right?"

"Sure," Cheng Feichi agreed, his eyes reflecting a vibrant green expanse.

They stayed in a hotel that night, in a top-floor suite where Cheng Feichi often stayed.

Now that they'd settled down in the capital and often visited Yi Hui in the city, Ye Qin had placed "buying property in S-City" on their agenda. They agreed he would buy the house this time, and Cheng Feichi just needed to move in with his bags.

While the hotel was decent, the bathroom was too small and could only accommodate one person at a time, which made *certain* activities inconvenient.

Cheng Feichi stepped into the bedroom after his shower and saw Ye Qin stuffing something under the pillow in a fluster. When Ye Qin took his turn in the bathroom, Cheng Feichi leaned back on the bed and "accidentally" brushed his hand against the photo album that had slipped out from under the pillow. Since it'd delivered itself to his hands, he might as well look through it. Besides, it wasn't the first time he'd seen Ye Qin fiddling with it. He was curious about the secrets contained within this rose-colored album.

He was taken by surprise when he opened the first page.

It was a photo of himself at eighteen, with a flustered expression that clearly belonged to one who was unaccustomed to having his photo taken and was caught off guard by the camera.

He thought this photo was a thing of the past, existing only in that now-outdated phone. He never expected Ye Qin to hold on to it until now; Ye Qin had even printed and preserved it.

The rest of the photos were all of him. The first half was digital snapshots printed on regular photo paper, but starting from the end of last year, those gave way to Polaroid prints. The first was taken during the first snow. Cheng Feichi, who had been

standing by the window, had turned around just in time to face the camera and the radiant smile of the person behind the lens.

Even the photos taken at Disneyland earlier had been added, with the date noted in the blank space, followed by a crooked line that said: *From now on, we're going to spend every birthday together.*

What Ye Qin didn't know was that Cheng Feichi had a similar photo album too, except his was on his phone and custom-sorted. The first was an image saved from the internet, showing an eight-year-old Ye Qin playing the piano at a youth cultural performance. The second was a dated and blurry high school ID photo of Ye Qin flashing his two tiny canine teeth, completed with a stubborn lock of hair sticking up on his head.

The photos that came after had never been seen by anyone other than Cheng Feichi himself.

There were photos taken at school: Ye Qin gnawing on pork ribs; Ye Qin yawning as he stood in line during physical education class; Ye Qin pushing his bike as he walked ahead after evening self-study sessions. Cheng Feichi had just put away his phone when Ye Qin turned around and urged him on, *"Hurry up!"*

Then there were also those from the time they lived together at Jiayuan Compound: Ye Qin sulking with puffed-up cheeks after losing a game; Ye Qin solemnly holding up a freshly-washed shirt to check if it was clean after he'd just learned to use the washing machine; and Ye Qin sleeping at the study table they shared during a revision session, his cheek pressed against a practice quiz paper.

The ones later were even more private and intimate: Ye Qin laughing heartily as he held up their marriage certificate; Ye Qin figuring out how to tie the belt of his new pajamas; Ye Qin pulling the curtains open one morning, his face bathed in the first ray of sunlight. There was also a short video of him secretly

practicing his dance moves at home one rainy day.

There were even screenshots taken from video calls when they were apart, showing Ye Qin with a deliberately opened collar that revealed his slender neck and defined collarbones, blushing as he asked, *"When will you be back?"*

The latest one showed a slender and fair arm, with a silver bracelet formed out of countless diamond flowers lying across the prominent wrist, as dazzling as clear spring water flowing through fresh snow.

That was from November 29th last year. A Harry Winston Sunflower bracelet that Cheng Feichi gave to Ye Qin as a birthday gift, other than the homemade cake.

Ye Qin loved it very much and wore it whenever he didn't have to attend public events. When he first received it, he ran his fingers over the flower petals and asked Cheng Feichi with a tilt of his head, "It's a sunflower, right?"

Of course, no flower in the world could be as radiant as the one Cheng Feichi possessed.

Cheng Feichi moved the new photos taken today to the photo album named *Sunflower*, exited, and locked his phone. Finally, he pushed Ye Qin's photo album back into its hiding place under the pillow.

Actually, he didn't need all of these to prove anything.

Because *his* sunflower had already bloomed in his heart.

"Happy birthday!"

"Mn."

"And...I love you so much!"

"I love you too."

EXTRA 21

First Love

COME midsummer, Ye Qin joined a drama production and started filming.

It was an idol drama set on campus. The male lead was a rising star, while the female lead was Liu Yuqing, an old acquaintance. Once again, Ye Qin played the role of her younger brother.

A month after the shooting began, Liao Yifang dropped by the set for a visit. When Ye Qin returned to the side after completing a scene, he saw Liao Yifang craning his neck to observe the male and female lead filming an intimate scene under the parasol tree.

Ye Qin followed his gaze and took a swig of mineral water. "Enjoying the view?"

Liao Yifang snapped out of his thoughts, looking a little bashful. "No... It just reminded me of our school days."

Ye Qin watched the scene on the other side and blurted in astonishment, "Don't tell me Zhou Feng did...that to you in school?"

Looking even more embarrassed now, Liao Yifang waved his hands. "No, no. We just...held hands during late-night self-study when no one was around."

"And here I thought only Zhou Feng would be thick-skinned enough to... Who would have guessed you to have it in you, too?"

As he spoke, he belatedly processed the keyword *late-night self-study,* triggering a memory of his own first clandestine encounter in the shadows of the classroom during a power outage one night.

Mortified, Liao Yifang took a sip of water and glanced at Ye Qin. "Huh? Why are your ears red?"

Ye Qin couldn't possibly tell the truth, so he nonchalantly rubbed his thin-skinned cheeks and made a show of snapping a photo of the male lead. "I just realized he's really quite handsome."

That evening, as the two of them ate at a restaurant near the film set, Liao Yifang's phone rang. He answered to Zhou Feng's booming voice demanding to know where he was and when he would be home. His appetite gone, Liao Yifang set down his chopsticks to leave.

Exasperated, Ye Qin called Zhou Feng and reproached him. "He rarely comes to see me. Why are you in such a hurry to rush him home? Worried I'll devour him whole?"

Zhou Feng sounded quite aggrieved. "It's not you I'm worried about. But if he stays any longer, he might just end up being bewitched."

His words puzzled Ye Qin, who finally understood when he scrolled through his social media feed later while waiting for his next scene—Liao Yifang had posted a new update that afternoon with a profile shot of the male lead taken at the set, captioned: *Ye Qin says he's handsome. On closer look, that's indeed the case.*

Indeed.

Ye Qin thought. *If I were Zhou Feng, I'd be worried about some temptress out there seducing my wife. I'd want to keep him*

close, too.

With that thought, Ye Qin switched back to the chat interface, clicked on the profile picture for one of the pinned conversations, and scrolled through the person's social media feed. It hadn't been updated in half a year. He pursed his lip, feeling reassured and oddly disappointed.

Had he been in Liao Yifang's shoes, Cheng Feichi would have been totally cool and indifferent about it.

Ye Qin tossed the phone on the table and stretched lazily while letting loose a long sigh.

It had been half a month since they last saw each other.

There was a water rescue scene that evening. Ye Qin, who didn't have a stunt double, took three takes before the shots were approved.

Fortunately, the weather was hot, and the river water wasn't too cold. After getting out of the water, Ye Qin wrapped the blanket the assistant handed him around himself and announced with a flip of his hair. "Time to clock out!"

On the way back to the hotel, Ye Qin picked up his phone and saw a message Cheng Feichi had sent him an hour before asking when he'd be done.

Although they were often apart, they would video-call each other every day, no matter how late. So Ye Qin found nothing odd about this and answered: *[Otw! See u in 5! (｡•̀ ᵕ－)✧]*

However, the "see you" wasn't through a screen as he'd expected.

When he swiped his card and opened the door to his room, he found the entryway lights on, but it didn't dawn on him until the man sitting at the desk stood up and turned around. His eyes widened with recognition, and he practically dashed over and threw himself into the man's arms.

"What are you doing here?" Ye Qin exclaimed in surprise and delight.

Cheng Feichi didn't answer him but caught him in his arms. Feeling the dampness in his hair, he furrowed his brows and herded him into the bathroom. With a hand, he grabbed a towel and draped it over Ye Qin's head.

Relishing the long overdue hair-drying service, Ye Qin grinned, his eyes curving into crescents. Cheng Feichi caught his expression in the mirror.

When asked what he was smiling about, Ye Qin's grin widened. "I'm happy." As for the source of his delight, that was clear for all to see.

His happiness was so infectious that Cheng Feichi's lips curved into a smile, too. Without waiting for Ye Qin's hair to dry completely, he tossed the towel aside and cupped a hand around Ye Qin's soft and supple nape. Leaning in, he kissed those luscious lips that were always tempting him through their video calls.

The hotel rooms the production team booked weren't all that great, but it had one advantage—the bathroom was spacious.

Ye Qin and Cheng Feichi lingered in there for quite a long time, and Ye Qin even had to be carried out of the bathroom when they were done.

Ye Qin signed with contentment as he sank into the soft bedding. "Didn't you say you were busy lately? How did you find the time to come over?"

Cheng Feichi was even multitasking during their video call yesterday, his eyes so glued to the computer screen that he didn't even look up at him.

"It's true I'm busy," Cheng Feichi said.

Having been together for so long, they were familiar with

each other's habits like the back of their hands, so Ye Qin instantly noticed something off with Cheng Feichi's evasive answer.

Since he wouldn't answer, Ye Qin guessed, "Hm... Because your meeting was canceled? But it's Tuesday tomorrow, so there's no meeting... Or because tomorrow is Qixi? But didn't we agree not to join in the hype? It's so hard to book a reservation at a restaurant."

Seeing as Ye Qin was already thinking about tomorrow's plan, Cheng Feichi said, "No need for reservation. We can just grab something. I'm leaving at noon tomorrow."

"So soon?" Ye Qin mumbled and turned to look at the man sitting on the bed. "What are you looking at?"

"Nothing." Cheng Feichi closed the script in his hands and returned it to the bedside table.

His curiosity piqued, Ye Qin bolted from bed and grabbed the script. He flipped to the page where Cheng Feichi had been reading. It featured a scene where the male and female leads, who could no longer hold back their feelings for each other, finally embraced and kissed under the parasol tree on campus.

Ye Qin's reactions went from puzzlement to contemplation and finally realization as he remembered that Cheng Feichi had also added Liao Yifang as a contact on WeChat, which meant he could also see the latter's social media post from earlier that afternoon.

Was he jealous?

No way. Ye Qin's heart pounded. How could someone as steady as Cheng Feichi get jealous?

But *what if*?

Ye Qin picked up his phone, accessed the photo album, and deliberately cleared his throat. "Wow! Look! I got a shot of the male lead in this picture!"

He snapped his head up and successfully caught Cheng Fei-

chi's gaze.

That indescribable look in his eyes seemed no different from usual, but someone extremely close to him would notice something off-kilter about it.

Ye Qin swallowed. With a mix of nervousness and anticipation, he turned his phone to Cheng Feichi. "Our male lead. I heard he's a rising star. What do you think?"

The amber irises turned a notch colder, the wariness in them now palpable.

Cheng Feichi hummed an acknowledgment and replied in a low, emotionless voice, "He's indeed very handsome."

Despite playing with fire, Ye Qin was extremely excited.

He tossed his phone aside and scrambled toward the edge of the bed. "You saw the class monitor's social media post, right?"

"You must have. Otherwise, how did you know I said he was handsome?"

"That's why you rushed over, right?"

"So you *do* get jea—"

Before he could finish his words, Cheng Feichi threw the blanket over his head and bundled him up like a dumpling. Throwing Ye Qin back to the middle of the bed, he said, "Put your clothes on."

"Nope. I won't. What can you do?" Ye Qin struggled to turn over and persisted, "Not unless you admit to being jea—"

He didn't get to finish his word again.

"You said you missed me during our video call yesterday," Cheng Feichi said.

Ye Qin was taken aback. "I thought you didn't hear me..."

Cheng Feichi kneeled on the bed and gently ruffled Ye Qin's hair, feeling somewhat ticklish from the touch.

He looked at Ye Qin with a resigned expression and answered

softly, "I missed you too."

Ye Qin instantly melted.

He struggled to free his arms to hug Cheng Feichi and nuzzled against his neck, calling him softly and repeating how much he missed him during filming, eating, and especially in the quiet of the night. He missed him so much that he almost cried.

Cheng Feichi scrolled to the photo of the male lead taken that afternoon and half-jokingly quipped, "So much for missing me, huh?"

Ye Qin snatched his phone back and deleted the photo right before Cheng Feichi. "When I took this photo, I was actually thinking, how can he be compared to you? He's not even a fraction as handsome as you," he said in all seriousness.

Cheng Feichi blurted out laughing at his exaggerated description—although it wasn't an exaggeration at all.

The next day, Ye Qin returned to the film set after seeing Cheng Feichi off. Liu Yuqing winked knowingly at him, as if to say, "I knew you must have had a passionate time last night."

Embarrassed, Ye Qin pulled his collar higher and took a big gulp of water.

Liu Yuqing came over and nudged him with her elbow. "Say, I have a question for you."

"...What?"

"It's been a long time since I left school life, and I'm out of my element here.... Both of you have experience with first love. So why don't you tell me how you fell for him?"

Looking back now, Ye Qin actually wasn't sure when exactly he'd fallen for Cheng Feichi, but he'd always remember that moment—a bright summer day; a shady path outside the school campus; a speeding bicycle; and the tall, slim silhouette

of a young man.

A breeze blew past then, sending the trees rustling and the young man's school T-shirt billowing. Ye Qin involuntarily tightened his grip on the fabric, as if by doing so, he could conceal the clamorous pounding of his heart.

He looked up from where he was in the back seat. The young man turned back, his handsome profile smiling as the sunlight danced through his fluttering black hair.

"We're almost there," the young man reassured him, thinking Ye Qin was uncomfortable in the back seat.

Ye Qin subconsciously shook his head, thinking how wonderful it'd be if this road never ended.

Later, when asked the same question about when he first felt the stirring of love, Cheng Feichi couldn't give a definitive answer either.

What he vividly remembered was the glimpse of that familiar figure when he was working part-time at the restaurant. He'd chased after him without even giving it a second thought, but he didn't manage to catch up, and the fear and regret of letting something slip him by seized him.

Before that, Cheng Feichi had just witnessed Ye Qin wiping away tears of disappointment when he didn't get to sit beside him on the bus. That was when he realized there was someone in this world who could unnerve him and command all his attention, all without a single word ever being spoken.

It was how he learned many things about Ye Qin that no one else knew, like how he liked drinking sweet fruit juices, especially snow pear with rock sugar, or how he would puff up his cheeks when he was unhappy, roll his eyes when he was exasperated, or glance around nervously and chug water in a rather conspicuous attempt to hide it when he was shy. And how he was always so

dauntless but would transform into a docile cat whenever he saw Cheng Feichi, always blushing, acting like a spoiled, pampered child.

Many quiet afternoons, Ye Qin would sleep soundly in the corner of the classroom, while Cheng Feichi would have his pen in his hand and his workbook open in front of him. Unable to focus, he would soundlessly reach out to touch Ye Qin's hair before quickly pulling back. Even if these feelings felt unfamiliar and vague, Cheng Feichi knew it was the desire to get closer; he couldn't help himself.

So, time was actually a good thing.

Not only could it heal wounds, it could also make wonderful memories come into clear focus, so that they sparkle like gemstones.

Fearing he might forget what happened on the eve of Qixi, Ye Qin immediately jotted it down, turning it into a short essay.

Title: A Day in the Life of A Jealous Cheng Feichi.

Cheng Feichi left a comment after reading it: *some content doesn't match the facts.*

Disagreeing, Ye Qin fluttered his eyes rapidly at Cheng Feichi. "Are you sure? Think again?"

Unable to withstand such a tactic, Cheng Feichi personally deleted the comment, which meant the essay was factually accurate.

"Um..."

"Hm?"

"Am I your first love?"

"What do you think?"

"I want to hear you say it."

"Uh-huh."

"What does 'uh-huh' mean?"

"You're the only one."

"Hehe."

"What does 'hehe' mean?"

"It means 'it was the same for me."

"Um...I really like seeing you getting jealous."

"What?"

"Can you get jealous more often in the future?"

"Nope."

"Okay, then I will."

"...Don't."

"Why?"

"Because that's just borrowing trouble."

"Oh, so you do know it's borrowing trouble."

"Meh."

Ye Qin thought Cheng Feichi was really a very stable person. Consequently, he occasionally lacked passion and novelty in his life. But that didn't stop him from having the best first love in the world. It was an earth-shaking experience, with ripples of after-shocks that lingered afterward. If there had to be an embodiment of his first love, it'd be the shared morning and exchange of good-night for countless days and nights to come.

"Um..."

"Go to sleep. Don't you need to wake up early tomorrow?"

"All right then. Let's have breakfast together tomorrow."

"Okay."

"Good night, Cheng Feichi."

"Good night, Ye Xiaoruan."

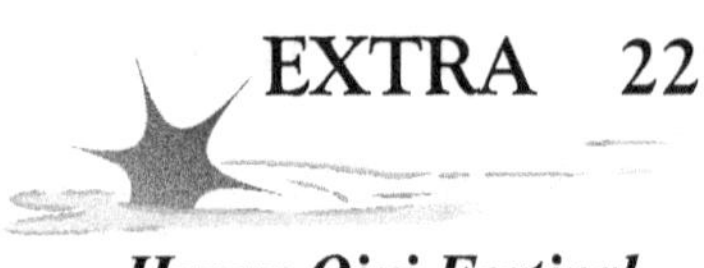

EXTRA 22

Happy Qixi Festival

1.

After playing the role of a younger brother for the nth time, Ye Qin finally got a role with a different character design: a young man who endured humiliation and stayed by his enemy's side, biding his time for revenge. He'd wear a smile before his enemy, letting the hatred and malice surface in his eyes only when he was alone.

Smiling was the easy part, but the vicious glares proved to be a problem for Ye Qin.

Ye Qin, who hoped to break away from his established image and label of a typecast actor, cherished this opportunity greatly. Before joining the production, he'd watched a dozen similar films to study characters with the same background.

It stood to reason that he also needed someone to rehearse with.

His first choice was the person closest to him—Cheng Feichi. But Cheng Feichi, who played the role of Ye Qin's enemy, had only just spoken two lines when Ye Qin frantically waved his hands in surrender. "No, no. This won't do. I get so incredibly happy whenever I see you; I can't hate you at all."

So, he switched partners to Zhou Feng, who just had his

216

hair cut by Liao Yifang. The class monitor was still as committed as ever to saving money, but alas, his haircutting skills hadn't improved in the slightest. Even if Ye Qin could summon up the hatred with his eyes closed, he only had to catch sight of Zhou Feng's bald patch and he would break out in a grin.

At the end of his tether, Zhou Feng discussed with Liao Yifang and came up with a trick that was guaranteed to incur Ye Qin's wrath—by changing the line to: *You know what? Cheng Feichi isn't all that handsome after all.*

That stunned Ye Qin, and his eyes soon blazed with fury as he hissed through clenched teeth, "Say that again if you dare!"

2.

Ye Qin had a guest appearance on a live stream on the night of the Qixi festival. But as he'd stayed up late filming yesterday and was in a hurry to rush back home today, he was a little distracted. Only when it was time to promote a hotel's vacation package did he perk up a little.

The host, having done their homework, cued Ye Qin while explaining the package and asked him to share his tips on choosing hotels.

Ye Qin held nothing back and spoke on everything from the differences between peak and off-peak seasons to choosing room types to weighing the importance of location and facilities. Each time the host read a comment from the live chat, he'd respond to them like a seasoned vacationer.

After he'd shared everything, someone in the comments asked: *how does Qin-Qin know so much about this?*

It was clearly from a fan, and the host read out the question.

Tired and parched from all the talking, Ye Qin's brain crashed, and he blurted without thinking, "My gege told me."

Thanks to the fans' explanation in the comments, everyone

217

who watched the live stream now knew that actor Ye Qin's partner was the CEO of a well-known hotel group. And everyone couldn't help but gush over how romantic Ye Qin's term of endearment for his husband was, especially considering this was on a live stream during the Qixi festival.

It all spiraled out of control from then on. The fans went wild shipping them, and for a time, Cheng Feichi's name even trended on social media.

3.

Apart from the public announcement of their relationship, Ye Qin and Cheng Feichi tacitly agreed to keep their relationship low-key, not wanting to interfere with each other's careers. This was especially true for Cheng Feichi, as the public wouldn't care about his abilities and achievements; they'd only care about juicy gossip like him being "the illegitimate son of the Yi family."

Well, so much for keeping a low profile now.

When Ye Qin left the live stream, he did so covering his mouth, and he didn't let go even when he reached home.

Cheng Feichi had already learned of the "incident" from his assistant. He said nothing until he arrived home. "What happened?"

After hemming and hawing for a long time, Ye Qin finally managed to say through his fingers, "...You're trending online."

"Is that so?" Cheng Feichi said noncommittally. "What happened?"

So, Ye Qin summarized the situation. "I didn't do it on purpose," he said, feeling ashamed.

Even though it wasn't intentional, the damage was done. Ye Qin hung his head, looking prepared to face the consequences.

He knew Cheng Feichi wouldn't punish him, just like all those times Cheng Feichi never laid a hand on him even when

he told him to hit him after he did something wrong. So Ye Qin was simply going through the motions; he wasn't afraid at all.

But then a crisp smack rang out. Ye Qin snapped his head up in disbelief and reached back with his hands to cover his tender behind. "D-Did you just hit me?"

Cheng Feichi, who had turned to the side and was loosening his tie, cast a sidelong glance at him, as if to say, *Isn't this what you wanted?*

Dumbfounded, Ye Qin rubbed his buttocks, feeling that tingling feeling spread until he was trembling all over. His face belatedly flushed red.

It was truly a bizarre experience to be... spanked by Cheng Feichi.

"I never knew you were such a...meanie," Ye Qin muttered. The trickster kind of meanie, asking questions he already knew the answer to, and twisting the opportunity to suit his agenda. Heck, he even exploited his plight and spanked him.

After hanging up his tie, Cheng Feichi turned around and leaned over to place his hands over Ye Qin's hands, which were rubbing his buttocks.

"Really?" he prompted Ye Qin. "Think harder."

And so Ye Qin thought back on it, flipping through pages and pages of memories. Clues emerged through the overflow of tenderness: Cheng Feichi threatening to take him to the police station when he was caught keeping a lookout; Cheng Feichi deliberately leading him down a trail where he would be intercepted by the traffic police in an attempt to shake him off; Cheng Feichi pretending not to know him when he and the class monitor ran into him at the internet cafe; and Cheng Feichi bluffing him that he was "trespassing on private property" when they snuck into the repair shop at night... Come to think of it, the answers to that homework assignment that had gotten him

punished were likely problematic, too.

"Oh—!" It finally dawned on Ye Qin. "You were mean before, too." Most were to teach him a lesson or make him laugh, though, and Cheng Feichi had hardly put any strength into it, just like the spanking earlier.

However...

"I don't remember a single 'mean' thing you've done to me," Ye Qin said.

"Then what do you remember?" Cheng Feichi asked.

"I remember"—Ye Qin took Cheng Feichi's hand and locked fingers with him—"everything we've been through together." *As long as I'm with you, every moment, whether good or bad, is an exclusive experience you've given me.*

Cheng Feichi's heart softened as he looked at his reflection quivering in Ye Qin's eyes. Then again, he'd never been able to bring himself to harden his heart with Ye Qin.

Unable to wait any longer, Cheng Feichi cupped Ye Qin's face and kissed him.

As their lips locked together, Ye Qin heard Cheng Feichi say, "In that case, remember more."

Perhaps his voice was too soft, so soft Ye Qin couldn't tell if that was a request or a command.

4.

After tasting sweetness, Ye Qin egged Cheng Feichi on into being "mean" to him a few more times.

Cheng Feichi feigned surprise that there were people in this world who liked being spanked and asked, "Doesn't it hurt?"

"Nope, it's actually...you know."

"What?"

"...feels good," Ye Qin said in a small voice.

"What's that again?"

"...feels good," Ye Qin repeated softly.

"I can't hear you."

"I said, it *feels good*!" Ye Qin raised his voice in exasperation, only realizing he'd been tricked when he saw the upward curve of Cheng Feichi's lips.

He couldn't bear to hit Cheng Feichi, so he grabbed a pillow and pummeled it, cursing himself for not learning his lesson and catching on to the ploy.

After he was done, he flopped back onto the bed and calmed his breathing. Slowly, he turned on his side to face Cheng Feichi, his earlier feistiness gone as he asked tentatively, "...Do you hate me? Will you remember my bad side?"

It was his first time asking this question so bluntly, and he couldn't help but feel timid, so much so that he even closed his eyes for fear of seeing resentment in those amber-colored irises.

He heard a soft rustling sound, then a warm hand cupped his cheek, and a thumb gently stroked his quivering lashes.

"I've forgotten it all," Cheng Feichi said.

Encouraged by his words, Ye Qin slowly opened his eyes and met Cheng Feichi's gaze. He found himself drawn into those deep pools brimming with inexhaustible tenderness, and let himself fall into them, willingly surrendering himself to their depths.

In the quiet of the night, Ye Qin couldn't help but ask again, "What do you remember, then?"

Cheng Feichi chuckled.

It was the same question, and both of their answers were no different from each other.

I remember every moment I am with you—every single one of them.

And that—

"I love you."

EXTRA 23

Ye Qin's Birthday #2

1.

The first of November was All Saints' Day. Ye Qin donned his prepared battle suit and marched valiantly toward Disneyland, only to find out at the entrance that the All Saints' Day visitors weren't allowed to wear full-face masks. Left with no choice, he took off his Spider-Man mask and put on a regular mask instead.

As he took a few steps, he realized the lower half of his costume was rather tight, accentuating contours that might qualify as indecent exposure, so he borrowed Cheng Feichi's jacket and tied it around his waist.

Spider-Man was now just a headless upper torso. Ye Qin saw many girls dressed as princesses and felt a twinge of envy. At least they didn't have to wear tight-fitting pants or remove their headgear.

He still drew attention though, as he had been working out recently for his new role, and his abs were starting to take shape. That morning before setting off, Ye Qin had even complimented himself in the mirror, *"I can't believe such cool abs exist in the world!"*

Then there were his strikingly attractive eyes and brows

above the mask. Someone approached him for a photo and com-plimented him for being the most handsome Spider-Man. Ye Qin modestly deflected the praise. "No, no, no. I can't compare to Tobey Maguire, Andrew Garfield, and Tom Holland at all. Jake Johnson's voice acting is also amazing."

The girl asking him for a photo was taken aback. "I only know of Tom Holland. You're so amazing to remember the names of all the actors who played Spider-Man!"

Cheng Feichi, who was standing silently at the side, thought, *Well, you'd remember too if you watched the movies and behind-the-scenes documentaries a hundred times or so.*

Ye Qin returned home in a jovial mood. Before showering, he poked Cheng Feichi in the arm. "How was my outfit today?"

"Very cool," Cheng Feichi commented as he peeled an apple.

"Wanna see something different?"

Cheng Feichi stopped peeling.

Ye Qin came out of the bathroom wearing a Snow White dress and tugged uncomfortably at the puffy sleeves, revealing the red marks on his fair arms where the sleeves had dug into his flesh.

Then he picked up an apple and munched on it as he told Cheng Feichi about the embarrassing time in kindergarten when he was forced to play the role of Snow White. "The prop apple still had its skin. I couldn't bite into it at all," he said with calm and composure, but his ears had turned a bright shade of red.

Like Snow White, he didn't get to finish his apple, but unlike Snow White, who collapsed after being poisoned, Ye Qin was carried to bed.

Unfortunately, the dress wasn't of great quality and tore easily. Ye Qin felt a twinge of regret; he had been thinking of wearing it again next year's All Saints' Day.

When the deed was done, an exhausted Ye Qin quipped, "I

knew you didn't like Spider-Man, but princesses instead."

Cheng Feichi corrected him, "Only the princesses you play."

Pleased, Ye Qin said, "Shall we watch *Spider-Man: Homecoming* again? I downloaded the 4K Blu-ray version yesterday."

Cheng Feichi inwardly moaned to himself. There was really no such thing as a free lunch in the world.

2.

Back to that new drama.

Other than working out, he had to learn to swim.

It was hard to imagine that Ye Qin—who loved beach vacations, filmed three water rescue scenes, and even accomplished the difficult feat of retrieving a ring from underwater—was still swimming in the most basic doggy paddle style.

Not that there was anything wrong with the swimming technique. It was good enough for self-rescue under ordinary circumstances, but it just wasn't aesthetic on the big screen.

Cheng Feichi initially considered hiring a professional coach for Ye Qin, but Ye Qin declined and instead turned to free and quick online tutorials on Douyin.

He chose a hotel near their home. It was managed by Cheng Feichi, and he could freely use the huge, heated swimming pool without forking out the facility fee.

He spent a day learning to hold his breath and worked on the strokes the next day. He started with breaststroke, which the online tutorials said was easier to learn.

After swimming a couple of laps, he noticed a foreigner smiling at him from the pool deck. Thinking his swimming posture looked comical, he got out of the water and asked, "Excuse me, is my, uh, swimming form that bad?"

"It's pretty good," the foreigner said. "I can take a video for you so you can see for yourself."

Ye Qin was rather speechless at his offer.

The foreigner recorded Ye Qin as he swam, and Ye Qin returned the favor by filming him too. Realizing the man was quite a good swimmer, he took him on as his coach.

The man said he had come here from S-City for a business trip and had been staying at this hotel for a week.

Finding it coincidental, Ye Qin said, "My gege also frequently travels between S-City and the capital."

"Is your gege as pretty as you?" the foreigner asked.

Ye Qin took it as an invitation to boast. "He's so much more handsome than me! He's handsome whether he smiles or pulls a long face... but he rarely pulls a long face; he's super gentle."

A couple of days later, *super gentle* Cheng Feichi appeared at the pool, pulling a long face. "Ye Qin, get up here."

Ye Qin, who had been practicing swimming with the foreigner, quickly got out and wrapped a towel around himself. "What brings you here?"

The foreigner got out of the water too, but Cheng Feichi didn't even spare him a glance as he wrapped an arm around Ye Qin and led him away.

Puzzled, Ye Qin followed him to a private changing room and changed his clothes. "I'm not done swimming."

"We'll go somewhere else," Cheng Feichi said.

Half an hour later, they arrived at another swimming facility. Before getting into the water, Ye Qin asked in bewilderment, "Why are you mad?"

Cheng Feichi hugged him from behind and gave his soft waist a squeeze. Had he not arrived when he did, the foreigner's hand might have ended up there.

"You don't think there's anything off about this?" Cheng Feichi asked.

Ye Qin, who was slow on the uptake, thought back to recent

events and suddenly saw the red flag—the foreigner claimed to be in the capital on a business trip, yet he spent all day lounging at the hotel pool and even offered to teach him swimming for free.

So there it was—the foreigner was gay.

Realizing his mistake now, Ye Qin stammered that he didn't know the guy had ulterior motives; he just assumed he'd met a nice guy.

"Sure, he is," Cheng Feichi quipped. "If I hadn't shown up, you might have already learned to swim by now."

Ye Qin dramatically covered his mouth. "Oh, my god. Mr. Cheng's so mad his sarcasm's slipping out!"

Cheng Feichi was rendered speechless.

The heavy responsibility and honor of teaching Ye Qin fell to Cheng Feichi.

To be on the safe side, he bought a swimming float.

"Look! A float! We're saved!" Ye Qin exclaimed when Cheng Feichi returned with the float.

Cheng Feichi, who had been pulling a long face for an hour, finally couldn't help but crack a smile.

Relieved, Ye Qin entered the water with the float and used it as a boat.

Mr. Cheng got into the water to teach Ye Qin swimming. Ye Qin, on the other hand, came up with a new way to play: by using the float as a kickboard with Cheng Feichi as the propeller.

Cheng Feichi, himself an excellent swimmer, pulled Ye Qin along for two laps.

Enjoying the taste of this effortless swimming method, Ye Qin pleaded, "Can we do another lap?"

And then—

"Another lap, please."

"Again."

"Second-to-last lap."

"Last lap."

"If only we could do one more lap…"

"Imagine we could do yet another lap. I'd be the happiest guy in the world."

"I'm so tired…I'm gonna take a nap first."

"…Gege."

"Gege, gege."

"You're the best in the world."

"Can I kiss you?"

…

In the end, Cheng Feichi pulled Ye Qin around lap after lap, turning his already firm muscles rock-hard.

Meanwhile, Ye Qin barely made any progress in his swimming. But hey, as long as he didn't drown, who cared about aesthetics?

3.

When two people had been together for a long time, they would naturally come to discover each other's quirks.

For example, Ye Qin discovered that Cheng Feichi actually had some OCD tendencies: slippers had to be placed with toes pointing indoors; clothes had to be sorted and hung by colors and length; and he had to ensure all the doors and windows were securely closed every night before he could fall asleep.

Of course, this could be explained away as the habits of someone neat and tidy, but there was a time when Cheng Feichi left the bathroom after washing his face, only to double back to reposition the razor Ye Qin had casually tossed on the countertop, aligning it at a perfect 180-degree angle parallel to the wall.

Ye Qin had gaped at him then, with toothpaste foam still in his mouth.

The most ridiculous incident was when one side of Ye

Qin's nostrils had been bitten by a mosquito. He was anxiously wondering how to conceal this huge, red bump before going on camera the next day, when Cheng Feichi suddenly turned his face to him and pinched his nose.

Several seconds later, he let go, and Ye Qin discovered, upon checking the mirror, that he now had perfectly symmetrical red marks on both sides of his nose.

Even the handmade cake Ye Qin received for his birthday had a symmetrical design. To be sure, Ye Qin carefully counted the petals of the cream sunflower, coming up with fourteen on each side, totaling exactly twenty-eight. He even counted it thrice. Unbelievable—he was already twenty-eight.

And even at this age, he still needed someone else to tie his shoelaces.

One time, when they were going out, Ye Qin's shoelaces came undone. Cheng Feichi noticed it and grabbed him by the arm to stop him in his tracks. Then he crouched down and retied the laces with practiced ease.

It transported Ye Qin back to that not-so-cold Valentine's Day eleven years ago. A rose, a jar of stars, the same person before him, and the same pounding heartbeat in his ears.

Wait a minute—

It dawned on Ye Qin. "When you tied my shoelaces back then, it was because of your OCD, wasn't it?"

4.

Cheng Feichi didn't answer the question and simply chuckled.

Back to Ye Qin's new drama.

Ye Qin had to smoke for his role in the film. Worried he would get addicted, he practiced with low-nicotine cigarettes and strictly limited himself to a maximum of two per day.

As he took out the cigarette pack, a thought struck him,

and he asked Cheng Feichi if he smoked. He thought the answer would be a no, but to his surprise, Cheng Feichi glanced at him and said, "I used to."

Not the kind of social smoking at gatherings or smoke-filled conference rooms, but during his study abroad. Many sleepless nights, he would head out of his dorm by his lonesome self and light up a cigarette.

Ye Qin found it hard to picture Cheng Feichi smoking. Cigarette ash seemed too dirty for someone like him. It was also too rebellious and out of character.

So Cheng Feichi demonstrated for him. He tapped out a cigarette and lit it up with a lighter. Holding it between two slender fingers, he brought the cigarette to his mouth, closed his thin lips around it, took a slow drag, and exhaled, expelling a puff of white smoke that rose into the air and dissipated.

It was at this moment that Ye Qin was willing to admit that he had some strange kink, because the sight of Cheng Feichi smoking sent tingles of excitement down his spine.

Even so, he didn't forget to ask, "For someone who's a cleanliness freak, how can you stand the smell of smoke?"

The ember glowed in the darkness of the night, but even it couldn't match the intensity in Cheng Feichi's eyes as he looked at Ye Qin. "Because I missed you," Cheng Feichi said. "...I missed you so much."

No one could remain unmoved at such an admission. Ye Qin practically pounced at Cheng Feichi and wrapped his legs around the latter's waist. At the same time a pair of strong arms lifted him, he kissed down on those beautifully curved lips.

When Cheng Feichi threw him onto the bed and came down on him, Ye Qin was overcome by a brief moment of dizziness and a strange sense of premonition.

What was he to do? It seemed like he would forever be in

the thrall of this man, and all it took was just a single gaze and a simple phrase of his. And he could never curb his desire to explore this man's past, future, and body.

After they were done, Ye Qin lay on top of Cheng Feichi, panting slightly. "So why didn't you get addicted?" he asked weakly, referring to smoking.

"I won't get addicted to *anything*." Cheng Feichi paused before continuing, "Well, except for one person."

"Oh?" The corners of Ye Qin's lips curved upward. "Who is it?"

"His name is Ye Qin."

"Uh-huh."

"It's his birthday today."

"Go on."

"I wish him a happy birthday."

"...That's it?"

"Pass a message to him for me, will you?"

"What message?"

"I love him."

Ye Qin was practically beaming from ear to ear. "I think that's something you should tell him yourself."

And so Cheng Feichi leaned in close to Ye Qin's ear and said *I love you* twenty-eight times.

5.

His OCD is really something, Ye Qin thought. *When I'm a hundred years old and he's a hundred and two years old, is he still going to say I love you a hundred times? The sheer exhaustion of it would be the death of him.*

6.

Huehuehue, let's not talk about inauspicious stuff like death

and whatnot on such a wonderful day.

Here's wishing everyone many happy returns and may all your wishes come true!

Glossary

- *A-, Xiao-*: friendly prefixes attached to a person's name to show closeness.
- *-tongxue*: "classmate", added as a suffix to a school peer's name.
- *Ge, gege*: literally "older brother", but also used between people as a friendly nickname, or occasionally flirtatiously between romantic partners.
- *Di, didi*: literally "younger brother", but also used between people as a friendly nickname, or occasionally flirtatiously between romantic partners.
- *Jie, jiejie*: literally "older sister", but also used between people as a friendly nickname, or occasionally flirtatiously between romantic partners.
- *Mei, meimei*: literally "younger sister", but also used between people as a friendly nickname, or occasionally flirtatiously between romantic partners.
- *Da-ge, lao-ge*: literally "eldest brother" and "older brother, but also used as a friendly nickname between peers.
- *Laogong*: a term used to refer to one's husband.